"Rumours of these stories, ~~p~~ d live, had reached a near mythic level for those in the know, but not the GTA—those rumours pale to the notorious truth. Whether it's fruitcake zombies, overly possessive sweaters, or the holiness of a hockey arena, Bassingthwaite can skewer any tradition with Derby Cavendish's dry martini wit. *Cocktails at Seven, Apocalypse at Eight* is sassy, salacious, and superb!"

—Chadwick Ginther, award-winning author of the Thunder Road trilogy

"If H. P. Lovecraft, P. G. Wodehouse, and J. K. Rowling somehow collaborated on a book together, it still wouldn't be as weird, witty, and wonderful as Don Bassingthwaite's collection of stylishly silly stories. Defending the world from the forces of darkness with bravery, brains, and bitchiness, Derby Cavendish is the hero we've always needed *and* deserved!"

—Scott Dagostino, manager of Glad Day Bookshop and book columnist at DailyXtra.ca

FIRST EDITION

Cocktails at Seven, Apocalypse at Eight: The Derby Cavendish Stories © 2016 by Don Bassingthwaite
Cover artwork © 2016 by Erik Mohr
Cover and interior design © 2016 by Samantha Beiko

Distributed in Canada by
Publishers Group Canada
76 Stafford Street, Unit 300
Toronto, Ontario, M6J 2S1
Toll Free: 800-747-8147
e-mail: info@pgcbooks.ca

Distributed in the U.S. by
Consortium Book Sales & Distribution
34 Thirteenth Avenue, NE, Suite 101
Minneapolis, MN 55413
Phone: (612) 746-2600
e-mail: sales.orders@cbsd.com

Library and Archives Canada Cataloguing in Publication

Bassingthwaite, Don

   Cocktails at seven, apocalypse at eight : the Derby Cavendish

stories / Don Bassingthwaite.

Issued in print and electronic formats.

ISBN 978-1-77148-376-6 (paperback).--ISBN 978-1-77148-373-5 (pdf)

   I. Title.

PS8553.A823C64 2016   C813'.54   C2016-904207-3

                                          C2016-904208-1

CHIZINE PUBLICATIONS
Peterborough, Canada
www.chizinepub.com
info@chizinepub.com

Edited by Samantha Beiko
Proofread by Sandra Kasturi

Shelfie

A free eBook edition is available
with the purchase of this print book.

CLEARLY PRINT YOUR NAME ABOVE IN UPPER CASE

Instructions to claim your free eBook edition:
1. Download the Shelfie app for Android or iOS
2. Write your name in **UPPER CASE** above
3. Use the Shelfie app to submit a photo
4. Download your eBook to any device

Canada Council   Conseil des arts
for the Arts   du Canada

We acknowledge the support of the Canada Council for the Arts which last year invested $20.1 million in writing and publishing throughout Canada.

ONTARIO ARTS COUNCIL
CONSEIL DES ARTS DE L'ONTARIO

an Ontario government agency
un organisme du gouvernement de l'Ontario

Published with the generous assistance of the Ontario Arts Council.

Printed in Canada

COCKTAILS AT SEVEN, APOCALYPSE AT EIGHT

The Derby Cavendish Stories

ChiZine Publications

DON BASSINGTHWAITE

COCKTAILS AT SEVEN, APOCALYPSE AT EIGHT

The Derby Cavendish Stories

Good night, Buddy Cole, wherever you are.

CONTENTS

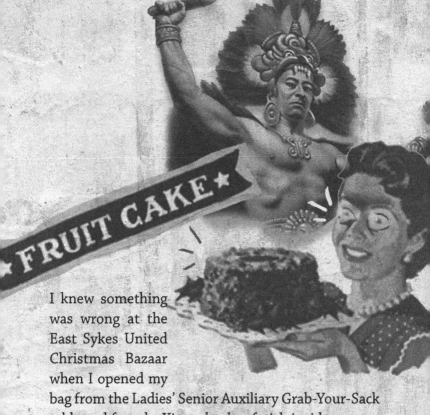

FRUIT CAKE ★

I knew something was wrong at the East Sykes United Christmas Bazaar when I opened my bag from the Ladies' Senior Auxiliary Grab-Your-Sack table and found a Ximec *huahua* fetish inside.

Fortunately, my trusted associate Matthew Plumper was with me. I grabbed him from where he was browsing the jams and jellies. "Do you know what this is?" I hissed, thrusting it under his nose.

Matt has extensive experience with things thrusting under his nose, but apparently a huahua fetish was new to him. His eyes crossed and bulged as he stared at the colourful ceramic stick, glazed as smooth and shining as a fresh Brazilian. "Derby Cavendish! Put that away!"

"Exactly," I said. "What is a huahua fetish doing at a church bazaar?"

Matt blinked. "A wha-what?"

"Hua-hua," I repeated, enunciating carefully. "A sacred artefact of the ancient Mexican Ximec tribe."

"Thank fuck. For a second, I thought you were waving around the world's ugliest pottery dildo."

I looked at the huahua, then at Matt, then back the huahua. "It's a fertility symbol."

"Oh my god, it is a dildo!"

"Ximec shamans used it to bring the dead back to life!"

Matt gave me a narrow glance. "How?" he asked.

I looked at Matt, then at the huahua, then back at Matt. "It's a dildo."

The poor boy's eyes nearly popped out of his head. "Do you mean they—?"

I put my free hand over his mouth. "Please, Matthew. We're in a church. And it's Christmas." I held up the huahua. "We need to find out what this is doing here."

The same experience Matt has with things thrusting under his nose, I have with the supernatural and otherworldly intruding on my life. They seem to be drawn to me. I've had to study them for my own protection—and for the protection of those around me. A huahua floating around without proper attention is as dangerous as a man putting on a dress for the first time: It may look harmless, but you never know how freaky things might get.

My old friend Edie North was working the Grab-Your-Sack table when we stepped up to it. Edie, a lovely old dyke, is the reason I come to the bazaar every year. She's laid more carpet than Home Depot but her face still lit up when she saw the huahua in my hand. "Derby, you lucky mincer! You got Faith McGilligan's fruitcake faddler."

"Her what?"

"Her fruitcake faddler. At least that's what she called it. She said it was the secret to her Christmas cake. Usually fruitcake batter can get too thick to mix, but her faddler made it easy. She used to say she'd never need a man around as long as she had her faddler."

I raised my eyebrow at her. "Really, Edie?"

She slumped a bit. "Lord, Derby, would you have wanted to tell an old woman she'd been using an antique dildo to beat her fruitcake for thirty years? Do you know how hard it was to keep a straight face while Mrs. McGilligan went on about how the bumps and ridges were there so you could really get a good grip?"

Matt giggled. I kept my face solemn. This was a serious matter. "She'd been using it for thirty years? And nothing unusual ever happened?"

Edie shook her head. "I'll say this: whatever the thing is, it makes for a damn good fruitcake. As far as I'm concerned, Faith was welcome to call it whatever she wanted. Apparently her great-great-grandmother was a missionary somewhere in Mexico and brought it back. It became a family heirloom, passed from mother to daughter. Faith cherished it like nothing else. Mavis Anderson asked to borrow it one year and the way Faith reacted, you'd think the thing came with a scrotum and a wedding ring."

I pounced on that little clue. "If she cherished it so much, why is it up for grabs at a church bazaar?"

"Ah." Edie's face fell. "That's the tragedy. Faith is gone—"

"Dead?"

I may have gotten a little excited. Matt elbowed me like a bride at a wedding dress sale and Edie looked appalled. "Moved! She retired to Fort Lauderdale last summer. When she downsized, she decided it was time to pass the faddler on and gave it to her daughter-in-law, Joy. But Joy didn't want it—she donated it to the Grab-Your-Sack."

"How come you didn't take it, then?" Matt asked.

"First rule of Christmas bazaar," said Edie. "Nobody takes from the donations." She wrinkled her nose. "Plus there were too many of us who wanted it. Someone would have noticed. Derby, if you wanted to sell that ugly lump of pottery, you could get a good price for it around here."

I squeezed my fist around the huahua. "I'm attached to it like it had a scrotum, Edie. But tell me: Where can I find Joy?"

※

It turned out that Joy was also at the bazaar, manning the bake sale. As we hurried downstairs to find her, Matt asked me, "Derby, if Mrs. McGilligan used the hoohoo stick—"

"Huahua."

"Whatever. If she used it to make her fruitcake for thirty years, maybe there's nothing to worry about."

That was when we turned the landing and almost tripped over a staggering man with cheap jeans and dead eyes. He might have been a husband dragged to the bazaar against his will, but there was something dark and sticky smeared around his drooling lips. Matt squeaked and pressed himself back against the wall. The man ignored him, swinging his head toward me—and the huahua stick. When I moved it, his eyes followed and he gave a low moan. I raised the stick high. He reached for it.

I kicked him neatly in the balls. I dated a soccer player for two months once and some of the things I learned then still come in handy. "Sorry," I said as he crumpled to the stairs, moaning more than before and clutching himself like he was looking for a prize. I grabbed Matt and pulled him after me.

"Oh my God!" Matt yelped. "What was wrong with him? What was that around his mouth?"

"Fruitcake," I said grimly. "We have something to worry about."

The bake sale was set up near the front door of the church, a temptation for anyone entering or leaving. We slid to a halt in the middle of it. "Joy McGilligan?" I called.

A sour-faced woman who didn't look like she'd ever had a huahua near her hoohoo glanced up. When she saw the stick in my hand, her mouth puckered even tighter. "Take that thing away! I don't want it back!"

I brandished it at her. "Did you use this to make fruitcake?"

She snorted. "Do you want some?" She reached behind the table, pulled out a basket, and set it down. It made a thud as if it were filled with foil-wrapped bricks. "Mother McGilligan swore by her faddler, but I tried using it and my batter just turned into a sticky lump around it. My husband could barely pull it out."

I had no doubt that he had trouble pushing it in, too, but aloud I said, "I understand the faddler was a McGilligan heirloom. Did your mother-in-law give you special instructions for how to use it?"

Joy looked at me like I was insane. "She said to only stir clockwise. How stupid is that? What difference would that make?"

Clockwise. From left to right. The path that the

sun follows from dawn to dusk. I drew myself up. "It makes the difference between life and death. Who has eaten this fruitcake?"

Maybe some of the danger had filtered into her mind. She looked a little frightened. "No one. We kept it aside in case we ran out and still needed something to sell. No one has eaten any of it yet."

"Oh, that's not true," said a sprightly woman behind the next table. "We took some of everything for the tea room. Plenty of people will have eaten it there—everyone loves the famous McGilligan fruitcake." She smiled just a little too sharply at Joy.

Joy glared back at her. "You're still mad about the faddler, aren't you, Mavis?"

There was no time for their petty arguments. I seized the basket of fruitcake, pushed it into Matt's arms, and swept from the bake sale back through the church hall to the parlour where the tea room was located.

My timing was, as always, superb. Just as we reached the tea room doors, they flew open. Terrified parishioners came racing out. "Call 9-1-1!" someone screamed. "They've gone crazy!" screamed someone else.

A teenaged girl with more piercings, heavier make-up, and a clearer sense of reality than her elders hit the nail on the head, though. "Fucking damn it, call the army—they're fruitcake zombies!"

Indeed they were. Standing my ground, I let the frightened mob pass by, then stepped up to the doors. Inside the parlour, a dozen of East Sykes United's fine, upstanding members grunted and moaned as they shuffled around the room. Dark and fragrant fruitcake smeared their faces. Tea and punch stained their clothes. Baked goods caked their hands. And I knew in my gut that at any moment, their craving could change from Christmas sweets to sweet, sweet flesh.

"Derby!" Matt whined. "Do something!"

One works with what one has. I raised the huahua high and I said "Stop!"

The zombies stopped—and turned toward me, their deadened eyes going to the ancient fetish. For a moment, they were still, awed by the power of the huahua.

Then they gave a collective moan and lurched toward me.

"Derby!"

I held out my free hand. "Fruitcake!" I ordered.

Bless Matt's flapping little ass, if there's one thing he does well, it's respond to commands. Instantly, a heavy package slapped into my palm. Without pausing to unwrap it, I tossed it to the zombies. They fell on it like paparazzi on a slipped nipple.

"That won't hold them for long," I said, taking the basket of cursed fruitcake from Matt. "Go back to the bake sale and bring everything you can."

"And then?" asked Matt.

I looked down at the fruitcake piled into the basket and an idea crept into my head. "Find me rum," I said. "A lot of rum. I think this cake looks a little dry."

※

And that was how the minister, the head of the Ladies' Senior Auxiliary, and half of the choir ended up being carried out of the tea room at the East Sykes United Church Christmas Bazaar suffering from alcohol poisoning and badly upset stomachs. One works with what one has and I had fruitcake soaked in enough rum to put the zombies down while I used the huahua to undo Joy McGilligan's unwitting curse.

Of course, no one at East Sykes will ever know that I saved the bazaar, Christmas, and possibly the world from a fruitcake zombie apocalypse. They blame it all on mass hysteria and rivals from the Anglican Advent Market armed with a tray of pot brownies. I'm happy to let them think that. There are some things better kept secret. Besides, I'm Derby Cavendish—and I know that I'm the meanest fruitcake there is.

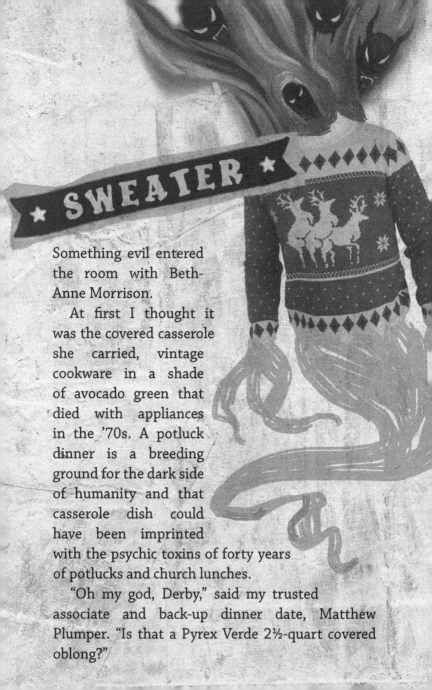

★ SWEATER ★

Something evil entered the room with Beth-Anne Morrison.

At first I thought it was the covered casserole she carried, vintage cookware in a shade of avocado green that died with appliances in the '70s. A potluck dinner is a breeding ground for the dark side of humanity and that casserole dish could have been imprinted with the psychic toxins of forty years of potlucks and church lunches.

"Oh my god, Derby," said my trusted associate and back-up dinner date, Matthew Plumper. "Is that a Pyrex Verde 2½-quart covered oblong?"

I know the supernatural and otherworldly. Matt knows his collectible kitchenware. "Matthew," I told him, "it could be a 2½-quart bed pan for all I know."

He gasped and slapped my arm in outrage. I kept my attention on Beth-Anne. The Christmas potluck is the highlight of the Bluewater Belles and Beaus Dinner Club's annual schedule of rotating dinner parties. No one wants to host an extra party in December, so the club gets together for one big table-breaking covered dish extravaganza. To be honest, I was only there because my friends Rick and Rick (or Ricky and Lucy as they like to say and everyone else is tired of hearing) were the new Bluewater chairs. I'd been dragged into joining up for the year, but now it seemed as if fate itself had called Derby Cavendish to spend his Saturday night in an overheated church basement. To my honed senses, the evil that trailed Beth-Anne Morrison was as obvious as bad tuck on a drag queen in a cheap miniskirt.

But it wasn't the casserole. As Beth-Anne set down her dish to exchange air-kisses with Rick One, the evil clung to her. Was it her hair, combed up and hairsprayed into architectural magnificence? Was it her holiday makeup, her cheeks like rosebuds, her nose like a cherry? No. I let my vision go out of focus, the better to see with the second sight, the third eye—or as Matthew calls it "that expression that looks like you're dropping a load in your shorts."

Dark shadows spread around Beth-Anne and the evil was revealed. It wasn't in her makeup or her hair or nestled among the shredded cheese, crushed corn chips, and refried beans of her infamous Tijuana Serenade casserole.

It was in her sweater.

I couldn't tell if the sweater was handmade or came from some godforsaken store, but it was an unnatural shade of green, the chunky yarn brushed into an imitation of evergreen needles and twined through with sparkling silver. It turned Beth-Anne into a walking plus-size Christmas tree complete with tinsel. I was surprised it didn't have twinkling lights, too, but then she pulled on her brooch and, lo, there was light.

Even Matt squeaked and turned away at the excess, but I studied Beth-Anne, trying to ascertain the exact nature of the darkness the Christmas sweater exuded—at least until Matt's squeak turned into strangled moan and he grabbed my arm hard enough to break my concentration. The shadows of Beth-Anne's sweater vanished. "Matthew!"

"Oh, Derby, you want to see this." He dragged me around with the wide-eyed lack of discretion that, along with certain other talents, has earned him the nickname Slack Jaw McPlumperson.

And for once, I couldn't blame him. Gracing the door with his presence, a big pan of kugel in one hand

and a bottle of wine in the other, was as handsome a daydream as ever stepped out of a Sears catalogue. Tousled blond hair, broad shoulders, square jaw, and fingers completely unhampered by a wedding ring.

"Dibs," I said out of reflex.

Matt pouted. "I saw him first. You were too busy admiring Beth-Anne's ensemble."

I bit my lip and looked back at Beth-Anne. It was the eternal struggle: battle the forces of darkness or rest my eyes on some juicy new eye-candy. And on second glance, the evil around Beth-Anne didn't seem that evil. She certainly didn't seem to notice it as she chatted away with Rick One while surreptitiously manoeuvring her casserole into a prime position on the buffet. In fact, I hadn't noticed before, but Rick was wearing a sweater that was very nearly as ugly as hers: sky blue with big golden bells and bright red ribbons. A sweater perfect for the co-chair of the Bluewater Belles and Beaus. I turned to Matt. "Let's find out who the new boy is."

"He's still mine."

"Runner-up can have the kugel."

※

With Beth-Anne's evil sweater still nagging at the edge of my senses, we went to the font of all Dinner Club gossip: Rick Two, a.k.a. Lucy. Somewhat to my surprise, he hadn't donned the obvious matching sweater to Rick One's. Usually they were the kind of couple that didn't feel complete if they weren't coordinating with each other and their tiny dogs. However, it was easier to talk to Lucy without being distracted by glittering yarn in mind-bending patterns. With far more tact than Matt could have mustered, I inclined my head toward the newcomer and said, "You don't see kugel at a potluck very often."

"It's refreshing, isn't it?" said Lucy. "So comfortable. So unassuming. It won't win him any points with the ladies who lunch, but when you look like that, no one cares what you cook."

"Who is he?" blurted Slack Jaw McPlumperson.

Lucy gave us a knowing little smile. "Let me introduce you." He led us to the end of the long buffet where the future Mrs. Cavendish was trying to squeeze his kugel in between Hamish Stewart's iron-tough apple crisp and Loreen Carmichael's sherry-heavy sponge trifle. The basement was getting crowded as members of the Dinner Club arrived. More and more of them seemed to be wearing hideous sweaters in all the colours of the season. Had I read my invitation carefully? Was there actually an ugly sweater theme to the party? How could I have missed that?

If only I'd listened to my instincts.

"Derby, Matthew," Lucy said, "this is Aidan. He just moved in up the block from us."

The dreamboat smiled and held out a hand as big and meaty as a Grade-A steak. While Matt goggled at the size of that mitt and all it implied, I seized the day and Aidan's hand. His grip was strong, his skin rough. While I'm not normally a gusher—verbally— it took a lot of control to keep my tone casual. "You work with your hands," I observed.

"Don't let the kugel fool you," said Aidan in a voice as rich as his hair. "I'm a carpenter."

The opening was too much for Matt to resist. "Oh, so you're used to handling a lot of wood."

Lucy and I froze in horror, but Aidan just laughed, a deep rumbling chuckle that rolled through the church basement and my lower torso. "I like you," Aidan said, wrapping a hand around Matt's shoulder. "Wine?"

The delightful tremors of Aidan's laugh turned into sour jealousy. He liked Matthew. Matthew?

"Well," said Lucy. "It looks like my work here is done. Has anyone seen Ricky?" He turned around— and found himself face to face with his missing husband. And his husband's sky-blue, bell- and bow-bedecked sweater. Lucy's eyes almost popped out of his head. "Oh my god, Ricky! What are you wearing?"

"Isn't it . . . gorgeous?" asked Rick One—and grasped Rick Two's arm.

This time there was no mistaking what happened. Even without second sight, I saw the evil that Beth-Anne Morrison had carried into the room stretch shadowy tendrils from Ricky to Lucy. One moment Lucy was wearing a trim burgundy shirt—the next, a sweater that was the twin of Ricky's.

And now the darkness was around Lucy, too. "It is gorgeous!" he said, then in unison with Ricky, "We're gorgeous!" They both turned to me. "Where's your sweater, Derby?"

I jumped away from their reaching hands and swept my gaze around the room. Had I really been so blinded by beauty and lust? Everyone was wearing the sweaters, even people I know wouldn't have been caught dead in more than one shade and a neutral. But maybe dead was exactly what they were going to be if I couldn't get to the bottom of this.

Aidan stared at Ricky and Lucy. "What the dingdong is happening?"

"Fuck dingdong," yelped Matt. "We're screwed." He wavered between hiding behind me or throwing himself at Aidan, then pressed himself against the beefy carpenter. I can't say I blame him. When you're facing evil, make every second count. "Do something, Derby!"

Faces were turning to us. We were surrounded. Beth-Anne stood behind Ricky and Lucy. Hamish Stewart, sweater embellished with a herd of reindeer in tartan scarves, closed in from the right. Loreen Carmichael, her sweater bearing a full-on depiction of the Nativity, including the wise men and their camels, came at us from the left. I held up a hand and invoked the First Name of Power.

"Armani!"

The darkness flinched back, then rose up. The crowd roared and surged at us with outstretched arms. I ducked away, pushing Matt and Aidan along, but I wasn't fast enough. Hands caught Matt's sleeve. He shrieked once before the sweaters swallowed him.

When the Bluewater Belles and Beaus parted again, Matthew Plumper wore an ivory sweater decorated with a massive ball of mistletoe. He raised his head and gave me a look filled with shadows.

"Oh, Matthew," I said. "I'm sorry."

"Fuck," said Aidan.

Matthew smiled at him. "I've got mistletoe." He ran his hands down his belly. "Want to kiss me under it?"

I caught my breath. Some small part of Matthew was still in there! There was still hope! "Aidan, get behind me and hold on tight!" Raising my arms, I started shouting more of the Great Names, battering the unknown darkness with their power. "Gucci! Prada! Lagerfeld!"

Matthew and the others stumbled back and I

dared to hope that Aidan and I might make it to the door, but suddenly I felt Aidan's powerful grip leave my waist. I threw a glance over my shoulder. Too late. Aidan wore a sweater, too, and to add insult to injury, it sported a mighty and virile candy cane thrusting up from the knitted waistband.

"Oh, bitch," I said through my teeth. "Now you've gone too far."

I stabbed a finger at Loreen Carmichael. "Kenneth Cole!" She gasped and staggered to the side. I leaped into the gap she left, throwing the Names of Power around like a cheap label whore. "Calvin! Donatella! Gianni!" I was at the long buffet table. I rolled under it, came up on the other side, grabbed the first casserole dish that came to hand, and lifted it high, ready to throw, as I howled the most powerful name of all. "Coco!"

"No!" cried the sweater-possessed crowd in unison. "Not the Pyrex Verde covered oblong!"

I paused and looked up. Above my head, I held Beth-Anne Morrison's Tijuana Serenade. Apparently that ugly avocado vintage casserole had more power than I thought. Advantage: Derby Cavendish. I scanned the room slowly. "Show yourself or the oblong takes a swan dive!"

The darkness shivered and drew together into a nebulous shape that hovered above the crowd. Big dark eyes stared down at me, glittering—and strangely sad. The thing's voice came out of the air. "I never meant to hurt anyone."

"Well, what did you want, then?" I asked it. "Look at these people. They can't handle this. Good lord, a bottle of sherry and this whole thing could get really ugly."

"I just wanted to enjoy a party. Is that so wrong? I just wanted to feel . . . pretty."

"This is your idea of pretty?"

The spirit bristled defensively. "There's a lot of love in these sweaters. Just because they didn't come with a designer label doesn't mean they don't have their own beauty." The possessed crowd shifted menacingly. Things might still turn ugly even without the sherry, and I didn't have the strength to take out the darkness controlling them.

I looked back up at the spirit. "What will it take for you to leave these people alone?"

I could swear that its shadowy expression turned into a pout. "I want my party."

Out in the crowd, Matt's face looked up at me. Aidan's, too. And Ricky and Lucy and Beth-Anne and all my friends. How could I let them suffer? I sighed and lowered the casserole.

"I have a proposition for you. . . ."

※

I don't remember much of the Bluewater Belles and Beaus Christmas potluck after that, but I'm told that after a strangely confusing beginning, it was the best one yet. Everyone enjoyed themselves— especially that nebulous party-loving spirit to judge by the taste of refried beans and sponge trifle that lingered in my mouth the next morning and the spare tire that grew around my waist in the week that followed. Yes, my friends might not have been able to handle possession by the spirit, but I was more than a match for it. I offered myself up to spare them. People tell me I was the life of the party. They don't know how true that is.

The spirit stuck to our agreement. It left me at the end of the evening's festivities and I haven't seen it since. With a few trips to the gym to restore my abs to their washboard glory, there was no lasting harm done—until Matt called me one morning. "Oh my God, Derby, they've put pictures from the potluck online." He could barely contain his laughter. I reached for my laptop and found the pictures as fast as I could.

I was in every single one. And in every single one, I was wearing a different Christmas sweater.

DREIDEL

Let it be known that Derby Cavendish is not one to hide the truth on the rare occasions that he makes a mistake. I have saved Christmas at least twice, but it was Hanukkah—Hanukkah with the Silverman family—that very nearly defeated me.

Nearly.

It began when my dear friend Aaron Silverman, a.k.a. Miss Mitzy Knish, a.k.a. the Jewish Hot Pocket, threw himself down on my chaise longue. "They're moving Hanukkah, Derby!"

I put aside my research on the legendary one-eyed serpent idol of Chakuja. "That seems unlikely, Mitz. Who exactly are 'they'?"

"My parents!" Aaron clutched a throw cushion. "They got a deal and booked a cruise over Hanukkah, but they still want to see the family, so they've moved our big Hanukkah dinner up by ten days this year."

I did some quick calculations in my head, converting Hebrew dates into Gregorian, then double-checking my work through the Julian, Sumerian, and Mayan calendars for good measure. Ten days before Hanukkah didn't produce any particularly auspicious or potentially apocalyptic dates. I raised a questioning eyebrow at Aaron. He shrieked and hurled himself back on the chaise. "It's my show, Derby!"

"Of course it is," I said quickly, making a mental note to stick the invitation in a more prominent spot on my refrigerator. Yes, after years of sharing the stage with other queens in badly lit bars and second-rate cabarets, Mitzy Knish finally had her very own holiday spectacular in a badly lit bar: THE LUMBER YARD PRESENTS GELT IN SHOWERS—A HANUKKAH EXTRAVAGANZA, BEST ASS CONTEST TO FOLLOW. "But that's not supposed to start until eleven thirty. Throw in the warm-up act and you won't need to be onstage until midnight. Plenty of time for a family dinner and a quick puke before you squeeze into your dress."

Aaron gave me a withering look. "What else is it?"

I thought again. Had I missed something? Feast of the Immaculate Conception? Feast of St. Eucharius? Sammy Davis Jr.'s birthday? (It's more significant than you think). Then it hit me. The Hebrew calendar is tied to the lunar year as well as the solar. Hanukkah begins on the twenty-fifth day of the month Kislev, when the moon is always past its third quarter. Move that forward by ten days . . .

"A full moon," I said.

"Exactly," said Aaron miserably.

When our Aaron was a young sprig on the gay bush, he had a life-changing encounter at summer camp. Two life-changing encounters if you count making time with his first boy crush—young Aaron really learned how to pitch a tent that summer—but more to the point he also got a rather nasty bite from something that the camp counsellors could never quite identify. Aaron was pumped full of antibiotics, his parents were called, lawsuits were threatened, and no one thought anything more about it. Until a couple of months later when the moon rose full and Aaron started sprouting more hair than most teenage boys.

Fortunately, Aaron had read his share of horror and fantasy novels—let that be a lesson to people who say they're a waste of time—and pretty quickly grasped that he had become *Teen Wolf*, Jewish Edition. There was none of the confused "Oh my

God, why do I keep waking up sweaty and naked and sexy in the woods when there's a full moon?" that afflicts people in movies. Aaron was already hiding one secret, so he just started hiding another, and while he eventually came out as fabulously gay, I was the only one who knew that his occasional need to get down on all fours and pee on things was more than just a puppy fetish.

Unless he gets really stressed, though, Aaron can control the change even on full moon nights. The launch of his show wouldn't have phased him, but his show and dinner with the family? That was a recipe for disaster.

"You could just tell your parents that you're performing that night," I suggested.

The look of horror on his face told me there was another secret in the Silverman family. "They still don't know you do drag, do they, Mitzy?"

"I can't tell them, Derby! My father is a doctor, my older brother is a doctor, my younger brother is a lawyer, and I put on sequins and shake my fake tits for tips. Besides, I have to go. My dad's family has a tradition of passing an heirloom dreidel along to the last unmarried child and my asshole lawyer brother tied the knot on a weekend bender in Niagara Falls last summer. This year, I get the dreidel." He sat forward. "Would you come with me, Derby? I need you to keep me calm. And there will be latkes."

One answers when one is needed. "Of course I'll come, Mitz," I said, but even then I could feel a nagging misgiving and not just about latkes.

※

Three things struck me as Aaron's father opened the door for us on that fateful night a couple of weeks later. First, that my nagging misgiving was back and stronger than ever. Second, that the Silvermans' house was so thick with the tantalizing smell of fried foods that I could feel my arteries hardening with every breath.

And third, that Aaron's father was completely shitfaced. I've known Dr. Silverman my whole life. He was my pediatrician and the first one to teach me—inadvertently and in a strictly clinical manner, of course—that warming up the lube before sticking it in is just good manners. I'd never seen him smashed before. Hiding my surprise, I offered him a smile and a bottle of wine. "Happy almost Hanukkah, Dr. Silverman."

"Derby Cavendish, welcome, welcome!" He took the bottle and studied the label. "Oh, now this is far too nice for us. I feel like I'd be the one giving this wine a hangover!"

He guffawed at his own joke and I let him have a polite chuckle. Aaron, however, laughed hugely, which seemed to please Dr. Silverman. He turned and ambled back into the house. "Sheila," he called, "Aaron and Derby are here!"

The instant his father was away from us, Aaron grabbed my elbow and whispered, "If he tells you a joke, just laugh! And whatever you do, don't let him corner you." He shook himself, stood straight, and marched into the house. Wary now, I followed him with caution.

Which was a good thing, because as we came around a corner into the living room, I felt as if I'd walked into an ad for some kind of Jewish spa. A lovely silver menorah stood on a console table, unlit in anticipation of the real Hanukkah, but a multitude of other candles had been placed around the room to honour the spirit of the Festival of Lights. They stood on coffee tables, end tables, side tables, mantles, and bookshelves; so many candles that it was a wonder Dr. Silverman hadn't already spontaneously ignited by mere proximity. I shaded my eyes against the brilliance. Aaron stopped at the door and shuddered.

"Hold it together, Mitzy," I told him. "Just imagine yourself on stage at the Lumber Yard belting out 'Oy to the World.'"

Before he could reply, the Silverman clan was on us.

Mrs. Silverman hugged me fondly. "Derby, it's

been so long. I have to tell you about our cruise. The deal was so good, the cruise line is practically giving the trip to us. We couldn't pass it up and I found the most adorable folding menorah to take with us. . . ."

"Sheila, he doesn't want to hear it." Dr. Silverman pressed wine on me and on Aaron, managing in the process to turn me to face a younger, more sober version of himself standing beside a rather dour-looking woman. "You remember Aaron's brother Ben and his wife Ruth. They're going to make us very happy about seven months from now. Another doctor for the family!" He elbowed Ben knowingly.

"*Mazel tov*," I said to Ruth.

"Don't patronize me," she muttered back.

I took refuge in my wine glass and quickly turned. Aaron's other brother, the lawyer, was there, smirking at my discomfort. He looked as plastered as his father, and if you knew David Silverman like I know David Silverman, you'd know that wasn't a good thing. He's slimy when he's sober and mean when he's drunk. Tonight, though, he just looked strangely smug. "Derby. Aaron."

Aaron's eyes narrowed in suspicion. "David." He looked past his brother. "Hi, Rachel."

Ah yes, David's bender bride. Maybe she was the reason he seemed mellower. I had to lean past him to see her and discovered a petite woman who looked more cute and less slutty than I would have imagined for David. She waved almost shyly and I smiled back. There was something vaguely familiar about her, something I couldn't quite put my finger on. I didn't get the chance to try again, though, as Mrs. Silverman reinserted herself.

"So the cruise has a fabulous itinerary. We leave Fort Lauderdale and visit Jamaica, the Dominican Republic, Cozumel . . . we're going to visit the ruins at Tulum and then go to a cocktail party on the beach—"

"We're going to have margaritas with the Mayans," said Dr. Silverman, and everybody laughed on cue. I caught Aaron's eye, grimaced, and gulped from my glass, which was probably a mistake as Dr. Silverman immediately topped it up again. After that, everything seemed to blur together as one Silverman after another tried to catch my attention.

"They have a surfing simulator on the cruise ship. Can you imagine me hanging ten?"

"You get the dreidel, eh, Ari? Sucks to be you."

"So when the doctor was called as a witness, he said, 'Judge, you're trying my patients—' No, wait that's not right. . . ."

"Have you considered the importance of getting your cholesterol checked regularly?"

"Of course, you can't light candles on the cruise, but we found these tiny, little glow sticks. . . ."

"More wine?"

"Have a latke."

"We're doing natural childbirth," said Ruth.

"Of course you are," I said. The leathery thing didn't look like she'd ever even taken an aspirin and as I watched her sip her water—room temperature—I couldn't help wondering what would happen if I slipped her some ecstasy.

Fortunately, Aaron wrenched me to the side before my bad self could speculate further. "Derby!" he said under his breath. "David just asked me what I'm doing later and said we should go catch a game after dinner. He knows about my show! I'm sure of it." He started twitching and his voice dropped an octave. That wasn't a good sign. I pulled him farther away from the others.

"Calm down, Mitzy. David is just a douche. He doesn't know anything."

Aaron gulped air and his twitching settled. "I think he does."

"How could he?" I looked over at David—and at Rachel, still hanging around him. Suddenly I remembered why she looked familiar. "Mitz, you said David got married in Niagara Falls. Didn't you play hostess to a stagette party there a couple of years ago?"

He looked at Rachel again, too. "You don't think? No. She couldn't be."

"She might."

"Oh, shit. Shit, shit, shit—"

His voice dropped deeper with each *shit* and I swear I could see his hair grow longer and thicker as I watched. "Easy," I urged him. "Easy! Just because there's a chance she recognized you doesn't mean she did. You've met her before tonight and she's never said anything, right?"

Aaron took a deep breath. "You're right. It's good. I'm fine." He took a sip of wine—

—just as his mother walked into the room with a big bowl. "Who wants some gelt?"

Wine sprayed from Aaron's mouth, extinguishing several candles and coating Ruth who let out a squeal and scrubbed frantically at herself as if the wine was going to soak straight into her blood stream. David started laughing, the most genuine—if mean-spirited—laughter I'd heard all night. Mrs. Silverman pursed her lips and started handing around little bags of foil-covered chocolate coins. "Ben. Ruth. David. Rachel. Yes, one for you, too, Derby." She stopped in front of Aaron, who had gone stark white, and reached down to the bottom of the bowl. "And a special Hanukkah treat for our baby!"

It was the heirloom dreidel—and it shone with a polished lustre in the candlelight. Aaron looked at it, then at his mother . . . then at me. "It's silver," he said.

"Well, of course it's silver," said his father. "The

Silvermans were silversmiths long before we were doctors. What, you thought it was going to be clay? Dreidel, dreidel, dreidel . . ."

Everyone else started singing along. I held my breath. Aaron reached for the dreidel, hesitated, then took it. Everyone except me cheered. I waited until Aaron looked up and smiled in triumph. No wolf. In spite of his family, the full moon, and a silver dreidel, he'd managed to control himself.

"Hurray for the baby," said David. "Let's eat." He tossed back the rest of his drink and headed for the dining room. The rest of the family fell in behind him with me and Aaron at the back of the pack. I leaned close to Aaron.

"Well done, Mitz. Nothing to worry about, right?"

Then we walked into the dining room, a flashing vision of silver and blue streamers with an enormous paper menorah hanging from the ceiling while on the table . . .

On the table was a centrepiece featuring a big photo of Aaron in full drag and a huge pile of knishes.

Aaron and I froze. I took me a second to register that the Silvermans had all gathered on the far side of the table—and that they were all smiling. Mrs. Silverman actually looked . . . proud. I glanced over at Aaron.

His gaze was locked on the knishes and he was shaking like a virgin in a bathhouse. The silver dreidel fell from his hand to clang on the floor. Five o'clock shadow swept across his face before my eyes, heading straight for a full-on beard. He threw back his head and howled.

I threw myself across the table. "Get back!" I shouted at the startled Silvermans. Standing on the tabletop with knishes squishing under my feet, I seized the photo of Aaron and spun back to him. A werewolf's transformation is not a pretty sight. Bones and joints crunched and groaned. Aaron's skull and jaw reshaped themselves into a muzzle. More hair than Whitesnake, Bon Jovi, and ZZ Top combined burst from his hide. At least the change was fast though, and in only moments, Aaron stood as a nearly seven-foot-tall wolf-man, his chest heaving and his claws digging gouges into the hardwood. Before he could do anything he'd regret later, I held up the photograph so he could see it.

"Mitzy!" I said. "Mitzy Knish, remember who you are!"

Aaron's eyes focused on the picture, then on me— and the rage drained out of them. For a moment, the room was silent.

"Well," said Mrs. Silverman. "I didn't expect that."

Aaron held up one massive hand, trying to hide his face. "Don't look at me," he said. "I'm an animal. I'm a monster."

Dr. Silverman coughed, then stepped around the

table. "You're my son—well, except when you're my daughter. Oh hell, what am I supposed to say in a situation like this?" He looked up to me. I shrugged.

"Keep going," I said. "You're doing fine."

Aaron's father looked back at his big gay drag queen werewolf son. "We were surprised when Rachel told us about—"

"I'm sorry, Aaron," called Rachel. "I thought they knew!"

"—but we just wanted to show you that we love you whoever . . . err . . . whatever you are."

Aaron dropped his hand and howled again, but this time it was clear that he was crying. He swept up the silver dreidel with one hand and pulled Dr. Silverman into a huge, hairy hug with the other. "I love you, Dad!"

Mrs. Silverman burst into tears, too, and rushed over to hug them both. Soon the whole family had surrounded Aaron in a messy pool of love. When they separated, he had shrunk back down to his normal human self.

Well, normal except for an astonishing amount of hair. The big problem with his transformations is that they always leave him needing a weed whacker and a full body wax. And tonight his timing couldn't have been worse. "Oh my God, look at me, Derby! I can't get rid of all this before my show!"

I hopped down from the table. "You know what

they say, Mitz. If you can't wax it, wear it. I think it's time for you to embrace the beast."

※

And that's how, a few hours and some fancy grooming later, "Gelt in Showers: A Hanukkah Extravaganza" went on stage at the Lumber Yard featuring a brand new look for Miss Mitzy Knish—the full-body poodle bob. It was a huge smash.

Mitzy's show and look weren't the only things to make their debut at the Lumber Yard that night. The entire Silverman clan came down to cheer her on. Dr. and Mrs. Silverman were the hit of the party. Ben picked up some new clients for his practice and even Ruth seemed to unwind a bit. Rachel did shots with some of the watching queens and found herself with a lot of new friends at the end of the night. David, on the other hand, managed to pick a fight after hitting on some of the same queens and was last seen trying to unwedge himself from a urinal in the ladies' room.

I had a feeling that Aaron's time as the only unmarried Silverman wouldn't last long.

NAUGHTY

I'm sure you all remember my associate Matthew Plumper. Matt is a dear friend and he's been at my side—or more often hiding behind me—through many dangerous situations. Against zombies, against demons, against hordes of shoppers at the mall on Boxing Day, he's never failed me. I may not let him play with fire after the infamous blue angel incident—I know he still regrets it, as do most of the unfortunate witnesses—but in every other situation, I trust him entirely. That's why when he recently asked me to help out at a fundraiser with him and his boyfriend Aidan, I didn't hesitate to say yes. Although perhaps I should have.

You may not remember Aidan. Matt and I first met him at the Bluewater Belles and Beaus Christmas Potluck—yes, that potluck—and he and Matt ended up dating. Which just proves once again that some people prefer a top shelf cocktail while others will drink screech out of a boot, but well done, Matthew. Aidan is a fine specimen: blond hair, broad shoulders, square jaw, and a carpenter by trade. And, as we discovered, quite the athlete. It's basketball in the spring, soccer in the summer, and football in the fall. Matthew enjoys the full benefits of it all, if you know what I mean. Aidan has arms for the NFL, legs for the Premier League, and the best basket this side of the NBA.

But his passion in the winter is hockey, and he's got the meaty ass to prove it. Imagine two beefy Turkish wrestlers packed into oiled leather pants and straining for dominance. That's Aidan's ass. And he's only one man in a thriving gay hockey league. Watching one of their games is like a sixty-minute orgasm with line changes and a referee. No wonder Matt has turned into quite the rink bunny.

Even the league's fundraisers are legendary. Every December, they take over the Lumber Yard for a night to put on a standing room-only jockstrap auction. There's very little sexier than a magnificently muscled derriere framed by a jockstrap and peeking out from under a hockey sweater. The auction is always a wild success—even if you don't have a winning bid, no one is ever really a loser. You can imagine my excitement when Matt and Aidan asked for help with it. It seemed like a good omen to find that the auction also happened to fall on Krampusnacht, that night when the ancient Yuletide spirit is said to roam in search of misbehaving children. Maybe Krampus doesn't get around much anymore, but there were bound to be plenty of naughty boys at the Lumber Yard.

So you can also imagine my disappointment when I arrived to discover that the league had decided at the last minute to try something new.

"A bake sale?" I demanded of Matt.

"Some of the teams said they were starting to feel uncomfortable. They said it was too sexualized."

"Really?"

Matt shrank back a bit. "They felt like meat."

"That's kind of the point!"

"It's not just a bake sale," said Aidan. "We have games, too."

"Are they sexy games?"

"They're bake sale games," he said tentatively.

I turned away in disgust, but there was no respite from the horror around me. The Lumber Yard had been transformed from a den of iniquity into a wonderland of sugary treats. Shortbread and rum balls. Fruitcake and sugar cookies. More varieties of gingerbread than I cared to think about. The liquor had been stacked away and the beer taps turned off while steaming pots of hot chocolate stood on the bar. The hockey players were all there in their team sweaters—but also in pants. One daring soul wore a kilt, but before I could thank the great spirits for small mercies, he squatted down and I caught a flash . . . of underwear! A gasp may have escaped my lips.

Thank heavens none of the auction guests had arrived yet or the league's fundraiser might have turned into a fun-drainer. There was still time to fix things. Something was very wrong at the Lumber Yard. The management wasn't the type to pass up a chance to sell hooch to an eager crowd and I couldn't believe that the same teams who had last year serenaded the crowds with a very interactive version of "The Little Drummer Boy"—not to mention such festive classics as "The Twelve Dicks of Christmas" and "Fellatio Navidad"—would feel uncomfortable this year. I really couldn't believe that Matt was capable of saying "sexualized" without giggling. Unnatural forces were clearly at work.

It was at that moment that Matt stiffened next to me and not in the good way. "Derby," he said, "don't turn around."

Well, what could I do? Matt might as well have asked a fish not to swim or a stripper not to grind. I turned around, of course. And I stiffened, too.

Walking toward us through the Lumber Yard, all attitude and eye liner, was a quartet of teenage girls. No, not so much a quartet as one supreme alpha bitch with her trailing trio of fawning bitchettes—a queen with her handmaids, a diva with her entourage, a cheerleader with her pep squad.

A cheerleader whom I knew all too well. She met my burning gaze and her cute little nose crinkled as she smiled. My breath whistled through my clenched teeth. Matthew grabbed my arm. "Derby, there's not going to be a scene, is there? This happens every time you two run into each other."

"She's a nexus of darkness and chaos, Matthew," I said. "She's evil incarnate in a mini-kilt and padded bra."

"Ummm . . . who exactly is this?" asked Aidan.

"Her name is Bethany," I told him without taking my eyes off her, "and she's my nemesis."

Matt sighed. "I don't know what's more disturbing. That you think you have a nemesis or that she's a sixteen-year-old girl."

"She's a lot older than she looks," I reminded him. "Do you really think a bunch of school girls could just walk into the Lumber Yard?"

His eyes crossed as he tried and failed to reconcile that idea with what he clearly saw strutting across the floor. Bethany's presence has that effect. Most people's minds simply refuse to acknowledge what they can't make sense of. Many pretend she doesn't exist. Some simply shut down. Some try to come up with any plausible explanation.

"They must have really good fake IDs," said Matt.

"Bethany and her harpies don't need IDs." I drew myself up and faced my foes as they approached. "That's close enough, Bethany."

"Derby, so nice to see you, too. Have you lost weight? No? Oh, you're just hanging out with hot people." Her eyes lingered on Aidan, producing a defensive squawk from Matt. Bethany laughed, a silvery tinkling sound I've always imagined to be the last thing mountain climbers hear as they freeze to death. "Easy there, blue angel," she said and Matthew flinched. Bethany flipped a hand over her shoulder. "Derby, you know my girls. Sara—?

"Ssssara . . ." hissed the willowy redhead on Bethany's left. Her eyes were like glowing embers.

"Rani—"

"Rrrrani . . ." growled the black-haired girl on Bethany's right. Her delicate nostrils pulsed as if she smelled something tasty.

"—and, of course, Cleo."

The girl behind Bethany looked as drawn and pale as age-yellowed linen. She didn't say anything but just smiled, her mouth stretching wide to reveal sharp teeth and black gums.

"Ladies," I said coolly.

Aidan, however, shuddered and shook his head as if trying to un-see what the strange world had put in front of him. "Let's go try out the games," he said to Matt, his voice on the edge of cracking. Matt hesitated. I knew that he'd experienced enough with me to resist some of Bethany's horrors, but his eyes were crossing again, and he was clearly leaning toward Aidan's denial.

"It's okay," I told him. "Go ahead."

His expression melted with relief, and he dragged Aidan away faster than a horny frat boy dropping his pants. "If you want us," he called over his shoulder, "we'll be at the cookie toss!"

With the two of them safely out of the way, I turned back to Bethany. "What are you up to, she-devil? Manipulation on this scale is big time, even for you. Have you got something against hockey in general or jockstraps in particular?"

"Unh—that they're both full of sweaty, hairy nuts?" Sara and Rani both snickered at that and Bethany tossed her hair back. "You're always looking at the small picture, Derby. Why do you think I'd turn this little auction into a bake sale? Why would I bother to come here at all?"

"Fashion tips and makeup advice?"

Cleo made a dry, rasping sound that might have

been laughter. Bethany glared at me. "I don't need makeup tips from you!"

"Well, not me obviously. Now Bruce over there, he may be a beast on the ice but he's a beauty in the boudoir. I'm sure if you asked nicely—"

"It's you, Derby!" Bethany shrieked, "I'm here for you, you meddling fruit loop!"

On the bar, one of the pots of hot chocolate broke with a crack beneath the blistering force of her anger, sending a steaming brown flood cascading to the floor. All around us, strapping gay hockey players froze for a moment as the slur pricked the surface of their befuddled minds . . . then slid away like the spilled chocolate. With barely a blink, they went back to ignoring Bethany and her girls. And, I realized suddenly, me.

Bethany must have seen revelation in my eyes because she smiled, her outburst fading like a fart in a jacuzzi. "That's right," she said. "No one to help you—just the way I planned it. I knew you wouldn't be able to resist an invitation from your little buddy Plumper and that as soon as you realized something was wrong, you'd try to fix it. And that as soon as you did that, people would start ignoring you like they should have all along." Her smile turned cruel. "You're alone, Derby. Alone and helpless. Get him, girls!"

Sara and Rani screamed and sprang at me like

animals, but Bethany was wrong—I might have been alone, but I wasn't helpless. I jumped for the nearest table, snatched up a plate of gingerbread snowflakes, and flung them at the girls in a shower of whirling, sugar-frosted fury. The damage was negligible—I mean, they were just cookies—but Rani got one stuck in her hair, Sara took another in the cleavage, and while they slowed down to brush out the crumbs, I turned tail and ran deeper into the Lumber Yard.

"Cleo, after him!" Bethany ordered. I risked a glance back and saw her third minion gliding after me, still grinning horribly. I quickened my pace. Chewed to death by monstrous predators in the guise of high school girls was not how I pictured myself leaving this mortal coil. I needed a plan—and help. I raced past hockey players who might have cheerfully body-checked my pursuers, but none of them even looked up. I needed people who understood what was going on, at least a little. I needed Matthew and Aidan.

But the cookie toss was already vacant and I could only pause to pelt Cleo with a handful of *pfeffernusse* before racing on and looping back up the other side of the bar. Bethany's voice rang through the Lumber Yard. "You're not going to get away, Derby! You're never going to spoil my plans again!"

"I do what I have to for the good of everyone!" I yelled back as I ran.

"Well, now your ass is mine!"

"My ass belongs to the world!" I winced as the words left my mouth. "Wait, I mean—"

"Too late!" cackled Bethany. "I'm already tweeting it!"

I cursed—but ahead of me, Matt and Aidan stood at another table under a sign that read SPRITZ FOR SPEED. "Harder. Harder!" I heard Matt say. "Squeeze it!"

"I'm trying!" Aidan said. "I think it's just too stiff to get out!"

"Matthew! Aidan!" I called and they sprang apart just as the cookie press in Aidan's hand finally oozed out its buttery dough. Aidan looked bewildered, but Matthew saw more clearly. He snatched the loaded cookie press from Aidan and hurled it past me with the practice of years spent throwing tantrums.

It struck Cleo right between the eyes and sent her staggering. I slid to a stop beside Matt, who glared at me accusingly. "I knew there was going to be a scene!"

"There was always going to be a scene," said Bethany as she stepped around the end of the bar. Sara and Rani were with her and they moved to cut us off from the side. Cleo had recovered from her blow. She drifted in from behind. We were surrounded. Even Aidan looked scared now. My mind raced as I tried to find a way out of this.

Matt, clinging to Aidan, gave me the answer. "You bitch," he spat at Bethany. "Someday, someone is going to give you the spanking you deserve!"

Bethany laughed her silvery laugh. "Oh, my little blue angel. Yes, I'm a bad, bad girl—but who's going to punish me after you three are gone?"

Inspiration struck me like light on a disco ball. "Now you're looking at the small picture, Bethany," I said. I stepped forward and raised my voice. "I call the Yule punisher! I call the dark goat, the black claw, the one who comes in winter darkness! On your night, O Krampus, hear and witness!" I pointed at Bethany. "She's been a naughty girl!"

It was an invocation of pure desperation, but I heard a tearing sound like the air itself was ripping apart behind me, followed by a yelp of alarm. The lights dimmed and the smell of green birch and black coal washed over me. I heard Sara's hiss, Rani's growl, and Cleo's dry rasp. Even Bethany looked startled. I turned around.

Krampus had come—in spirit at least. And a spirit needed a body. Personally, I would have chosen Aidan, but the blond bomb had collapsed into the nearest chair. Little Matthew Plumper stood as the vessel of Krampus. Curving black horns and shaggy black hair sprouted from his head. His eyes were red and his tongue lolled from his mouth, thick and mobile as a snake. His hands were huge and clawed and he'd grown at least three times his usual size, his clothes doing an Incredible Hulk shred—maybe more so because at least the Hulk's pants stayed on. If Matt hadn't been wearing an apparently very stretchy jockstrap, his tongue wouldn't have been the only thing lolling. Even so, I don't think anyone was ever going to call him "little Plumper" again.

Bethany recovered quickly. "Take him!" she shrieked and her harpies attacked. But Krampus was just as quick and fierce as them. He grabbed Rani as she pounced and stuffed her into a shadowy basket that appeared at his side. Sara swayed sinuously away from his grasping hand, but a hoofed foot swept her legs from under her and he popped her into the basket, too. Their snarls and hisses faded as if they were falling down a long, long hole. Cleo moved more cautiously, darting and weaving with quick feints. Krampus matched her moves, then, when she struck, lashed out with rattling chains that manifested suddenly in his hand. They wrapped around her and, with a heave and a snap, Krampus sent her tumbling into the basket as well. Cleo finally broke her silence in a terrible wail that echoed from the basket as she fell.

Krampus turned to Bethany but her hand snapped up, fingers spread wide in a gesture of warding. "You shall not touch me!" she said, voice ringing with power. "Not with claws or hands or chains!"

But I was already one step ahead of her. I leaped across the bar and grabbed a bottle of vodka and the long lighter that the bartender uses to ignite his signature cocktail, the Screaming Flamer. "Krampus! Catch!" I called and tossed both to him. He caught them, one in each hand, instantly chugging the vodka and sparking a flame on the lighter.

"Not with claws, not with hands, not with chains!" I shouted at Bethany. Her eyes went wide as she realized her mistake. Krampus dropped the bottle—

—turned around, bent over, and looked at Bethany through his legs. "Bitch," he said in Matt's voice—and stuck the lighter between his jockstrapped butt cheeks.

I've always said it would take an angel to stop Bethany. That wasn't what I had in mind.

※

In hindsight, I should have realized that Krampus incarnate was as much Matthew as he was ancient spirit. I'd thought he might spit a gout of flame at Bethany, but she'd goaded Matt on, so in a way it was her own fault. And to be fair, Matt had now redeemed himself for the previous blue angel incident. When Bethany returned—and I had no doubt that she eventually would—she was going to have a particularly ignominious defeat to live down.

But she was gone for now and Krampus, looking very satisfied, along with her. The only evidence of Bethany's visit to the Lumber Yard was a particularly greasy spot on the already stained floor. The last evidence of Krampus were Matt's thoroughly shredded clothes and his lingering amnesia. "Derby?" he asked "What happened? Where are my clothes?" He belched and alcohol all but condensed on his breath "Was I drinking? Why does my ass burn?"

"I'll tell you later," I said and patted him on his now-back-to-normal-size head. "But you did good, Matthew."

Without Bethany's influence, the hockey players swiftly returned to their senses, lost their pants, and the auction was back on, although there was a good deal of confusion about the strange proliferation of baked goods. Fortunately, I was ready with a suggestion and the first Gay Hockey League Jockstrap Auction and Bake Sale was a smashing success. In fact, it was their most profitable fundraiser ever—everyone went home with something to chew on.

Sometimes it's good to be naughty.

Pride is a wonderful time of year. A time to celebrate who you are, who you want to be, or just who you want to do. Personally though, I especially like Pride because it almost never coincides with those ancient dates of power that complicate other holidays for me. Christmas, Hanukkah, Halloween, Groundhog Day: I can't count the number of times I've had to deal with otherworldly forces when everyone else is tucking into a turkey dinner. Still, one has a duty to answer the call when it comes, although it would be nice if every once in a while that call was just for cocktails.

But as I stood at the corner of the Pride Festival's Second Stage, looking out over the crowd of happy fags and dykes partying in the street, I had a chill foreboding. Something was in the air and it wasn't just the usual complaints about the porta-potties.

A few weeks before, my good friend Aaron

Silverman had burst into my apartment. "They've booked me, Derby! Miss Mitzy Knish will be playing the Saturday Night Special on the Pride Second Stage!"

My first thought, as ever when Aaron announces a performance, was to check the date against the moon phase. Aaron isn't just the talented and fabulous Mitzy Knish, he is possibly the world's only drag queen werewolf, a combination that has caused difficulties before. But the full moon would pass well before Pride, so I had thrown my arms around Aaron and congratulated him. Everyone wants a chance to shine, but there are only so many spotlights to go around.

Still, I had to ask him, "The Second Stage, Mitzy?" Typically the crème de la queen play the Main Stage for the big crowd, while the Second Stage hosts distinctly B-list acts. For someone whose Hanukkah special "Gelt in Showers" packed the bar at the Lumber Yard and whose smash comedy showcase "Spit Roast" is still the talk of the leather men at Squeal, it seemed like a comedown.

Aaron had waved my concerns away. "This year the Second Stage, next year the Main Stage, the year after that . . ." He'd shivered and held out his hands. "I want you backstage with me, Derby Cavendish. A girl needs her support."

I'd protested—Aaron needed my support like

Olive Oyl needed a bra—but he'd worn me down with tales of after-parties with open bars, wall-to-wall go-go boys, and private back rooms. I'm not made of stone.

Except now that the night had arrived, I was as unsettled as a power bottom after curried lentils. I shouldn't have been. The Saturday Night Special was in full swing and Mitzy had already performed her first number, a mash-up of "River Deep, Mountain High" and "Proud Mary" that she called "Hi Mary," to great acclaim. Reining in my brooding unease, I returned backstage.

The bill for the evening was a veritable salad bar of acts from folk duo Jay and Wren, the smell of weed hanging in a fug around them; to Petal Marconi, a comedian who had probably emerged from the womb angry; to local piano-bar fixture Ricky Ivory, spoken word artiste Elsa Shush, and interpretive dancer Xabi. The organizers had dug up group acts, too: a trio of J-pop girls who called themselves, in letters and numbers, "CU2 Baby Baby," and an emo boy band, whose name might have been "Regret" or "Sad Puppies" or "Mom, the Cable's Out."

But if the bill was a salad bar, Mitzy was the bacon bits—even if she was still in her Tina Turner shock wig and fringed dress. "Shouldn't you be changing for your next number?" I asked her.

"Someone's hogging the dressing room," she said

tersely, the muscles of her arm bunching in a way that was more Beast than Beauty. Mitzy had tight control over the wolf inside, but stress and anger could bring out her inner bitch. I glanced at the curtained-off tent that passed for a dressing room.

"I'll deal with this," I told her, but she grabbed my hand and hissed, "Derby, no!" in the same moment as the stage manager, a harried volunteer named Shirley, called, "You're up, Hermione!"

A pair of sun-bronzed young men in tailcoats and thongs emerged from the tent and drew back the curtains over the door. The woman who stepped out was tall to start with and black stiletto heels added to her height. Silk stockings caressed long legs and lace garters played peek-a-boo beneath a maid's frilly skirt and apron. A corset pushed plump breasts into smooth curves nestled amid more frills. Her hair was pulled back in a bun except for two precise curls on either side of her dark, flashing eyes. Her lips, painted into a vibrant red rosebud, parted.

"I am ready," she said in a breathy French accent.

One of the J-Pop girls whimpered. The tall woman just swept past, although it did seem to me that she threw a disdainful glance at Mitzy. Her boys fell in behind her, one carrying a feather duster and the other a tastefully decorated spanking paddle. As they disappeared up the stairs onto the stage, the theme from *Downton Abbey* began to play—only to turn into the distinctive opening vocals of "Any Way You Want It."

The spell of her presence backstage shattered. Petal gasped and groped for a cigarette. Mitzy grabbed me by the shirtfront and hauled me in close. "She has backing dancers, Derby! Dancers!" She let me drop. "I need a drag king, stat! Get me a lesbian, stuff some socks down her pants, and I'll take it from there!"

"Easy, Mitz!" I urged her. "Who is that?"

"Hermione Frisson," said Mitzy. "The hottest thing to happen to burlesque since champagne showers."

"Well, get changed before she comes back." I hurried her into the dressing room. "Don't let her rattle you—your act is tighter than your tuck. Remember, she has to take her clothes off to get a rise out of the crowd."

The words weren't out of my mouth before a colossal cheer erupted outside. Mitzy's lips pressed together. "It's a one-note act," I told her helpfully— at the same moment that the speakers echoed with the sound of a paddle slapping flesh. The crowd cheered again. I pressed my lips together. "What's your next number?"

"'Carwash,'" Mitzy said miserably. She held up a body suit with stringy rag mops sewn over the sleeves.

"Make it sexy," I told her and went outside to

stand guard over the tent door. Hermione's music transitioned to "American Woman." The other performers also looked uneasy. Elsa Shush and Xabi both kept glancing at the stage. Petal lit cigarette after cigarette. Ricky Ivory flinched with each thwack of the spanking paddle. Only the folksingers Jay and Wren, up next on the bill, seemed calm, but I suspect that was mostly due to a surreptitious toke.

"American Woman" screeched to an end and Hermione Frisson left the stage to wild applause. She'd shed her maid's costume to reveal a star-spangled g-string and pasties with red-white-and-blue tassels. Petal nearly swallowed her cigarette. Hermione strode to the dressing room as if the other performers weren't even there, but I stood my ground.

"Sorry," I said. "There's a lady inside."

Hermione's plucked eyebrows arched high and that rosebud mouth curved in a sneer. "There may be a queen, but there is no woman, much less a lady."

Her dancing boys, ass cheeks now paddled bright red, chuckled and high-fived each other. I drew myself up. "Among queens, Mitzy will always be a lady. Among ladies, you will always be a five-dollar lap dancer with sloppy choreography!"

Hermione's eyes burned and she flicked her feather duster at me, dislodging a puff of sparkling green dust. "Wait until the end of the night," she said. "We'll see who has sloppy choreography."

The dressing room door fluttered aside. "Pull in your claws, girls," said Mitzy. She stepped through the doorway, resplendent in rag mops and a blond shag-do. "Hermione, the dressing room is yours."

Hermione stuck her nose in the air and walked inside. She and Mitzy passed each other like society matrons who had discovered they were both fucking the same pool boy. I fell in beside Mitzy. "Nobly done," I whispered.

"Did you see her tits?" Mitzy whispered back. "Holy shit, Derby, how am I supposed to compete with those?"

"You've got great boobs, too, Mitz."

"Yes, but mine came in a box and I leave them in a dish rack to dry!"

My attempts to reassure her were interrupted by a curse. "Jesus Christ, those fucking potheads!" snapped Shirley. She dashed onto the stage along with the sound technician. I was suddenly aware that the mellow songs of Jay and Wren had fallen silent. I craned my neck to get a look and saw the folk duo leaning up against each other—stoned into slumber. They barely even stirred as they were manhandled off the stage.

The audience was already heckling the delay. Shirley pointed to Elsa Shush. "Get out there!"

The spoken word artiste jumped for the stage and

the sound technician swiftly cued up her background music. Tinkling chimes and throbbing bongo drums swelled from the speakers.

"I stood on the roof," Elsa declaimed, "and watched the sun's setting cast indigo shadows across soulless condos where once . . ." She faltered and cleared her throat. "Where once bushes grew and sisters . . ."

Her voice faltered again and for several long seconds, there was nothing but chimes and bongos. The stage manager looked up with fear in her eyes, but then Elsa's performance resumed—sort of. It sounded like she was fighting every word that came out of her mouth.

"A lad lay with his beau by the fire,
Then succumbed to his lover's desire.
He moaned, 'That's a sin,
But now that's in,
Could you shove it a few inches higher?'"

You could have heard a testicle drop—then the audience broke into a mixture of howling laughter and outraged boos. "What the hell?" gasped Shirley, but Elsa was already fleeing the stage, wailing in shame.

My foreboding was back. I might not have appreciated Jay and Wren or Elsa, but they were seasoned performers and to fail so spectacularly felt downright unnatural. "Xabi!" called Shirley desperately. Chimes and bongos were replaced by wailing jazz horns. I took Mitzy's hand and drew her over to the side of the stage to watch.

Xabi burst out like a panther unchained, flinging off his shirt to reveal a tightly muscled torso. The audience cheered in appreciation and settled down, getting into the performance. The dancer's loose pants slipped to the ground. Clad in clinging trunks, he leaped in celebration of freedom and sexuality. The audience applauded and I joined in. Whatever had happened to the other performers, nothing was wrong here! Xabi's hands caressed his body as he moved, cupping his hard ass, tweaking his nipples, straying into his trunks. . . .

Mitzy's hand closed on my arm. "He's masturbating."

"It's interpretive dance," I said. "It's simulated. It's symbolic."

"No, Derby, he's really rubbing one out!"

I blinked. Xabi might still have been moving to the music, but there was no denying that he was now fully focused on his trouser tango. The audience had noticed too, and was reacting, as they had to Elsa's surprise limerick, with a fickle mixture of shock and appreciation. Xabi ignored them. He dropped his briefs and, no longer concealing anything, moved right up to the edge of the stage.

"He's going all the way!" someone yelled. The

crowd directly in front of the dancer scattered.

Shirley appeared with a big tarp in hand. "Help me!" she ordered and I vaulted up to join her. Together we managed to wrestle Xabi to the ground and wrap him up before the Saturday Night Special became an intimately interactive performance.

"I can't help myself!" he said, still squirming underneath us. "I don't know what's wrong. I try to dance and instead—oh God, oh yes, oh *yes* . . ."

But getting down and dirty on the stage had given me the perspective I needed. There was glittering dust spread across the boards—hardly unusual at Pride, but glitter that sticks in swirling lines as a furiously masturbating dancer rolls across it? That wasn't right.

"Shh," I said as Xabi gave a final shudder. "I know what's happening." I helped Shirley get him backstage; then, as the sound technician threw on dance music to distract the crowd from the latest calamity, I hoisted myself up into the steel frame of the rigging for a bird's-eye view of the stage.

The pattern in the glitter was impossible to miss from above. I slid back down to Mitzy. "It's a fairy circle," I said "Everyone who enters it is revealed for what they really are and their performances turned against them. This is serious magic!"

Mitzy frowned. "It wasn't here when I did my first number!"

"No," I said grimly, "I don't think it was. But I know where it came from." I bent and swiped my fingers through a bit of dust. They came away as green as envy. "Let's have a talk with Hermione Frisson."

Backstage, we found Shirley and the performers gathered together. The stage manager was trying to persuade the girls from CU2 Baby Baby to go on, but they'd dropped their cute act and were resisting loudly. I haven't heard such foul language come out of such small bodies since my elderly aunts forgot to fill their flasks before a dry wedding.

"But if someone doesn't go on, the show is over," pleaded Shirley. "We're going to have to cancel everything!" She looked from the J-pop girls to the emo boys to Petal and Ricky. None of them would meet her eyes.

At the back of the knot of performers, though, Hermione was looking smug. She'd changed into a sort of sexy Parisian cafe outfit with a tiny sweater, tinier beret, and impossibly tall heels. I knew in my gut that this was exactly the situation she'd been hoping for. With the others afraid to go on, she would take the stage as the star.

But before she could say anything, Mitzy stepped forward. "I'll do it."

My heart dropped. Shirley's face lit up. Hermione's twisted with rage. "*Non!*" she said sharply. "I will go on! Put this hairy penis out there and you'll just have another disaster!"

She was more right than she knew. I tried to get Mitzy's attention, but she wouldn't meet my eye. Shirley looked from her to Hermione and back again. "Mitzy," she said decisively.

Hermione screamed. "You're going to regret this!" she said, jabbing a finger at Mitzy and Shirley. She swept her hand around at all of us. "You're all going to regret it! This show will be the biggest failure in the history of Pride!"

She stormed away before even her boys could follow her. I grabbed Mitzy's arm. "Mitz, you know what will happen if you get into that circle. Everyone is going to see the real you." I mimed claws and fangs. "The real you."

"I can control it," she said. "Xabi and Elsa didn't know what was happening to them. I do, and I'm not going to let one jealous fucking diva ruin the show for all of us!" She slipped her arm out of my grasp. "Besides, remember what you're always telling me, Derby."

I sighed. "That you answer the call when it comes."

"That my act is tighter than my tuck!" She turned to Shirley. "Cue up my big number and give me two minutes to change!"

As Mitzy dove into the dressing room, I went after Hermione. The crowd was getting thicker, the audience swelling as word spread of Xabi's performance and people came to check out the train wreck of the Saturday Night Special. I could see Hermione's bun bobbing through the press of bodies and I plunged after her. Her exaggerated heels slowed her down and as she broke into a clear space, I was right behind her.

"Hold it, Hermione!" I shouted. She spun around. I stopped a pace or two away. "I take back what I said about sloppy choreography. Nice trick, working the fairy circle into your routine."

Her expression tightened. "I don't know what you're talking about."

"You go with that," I told her, "but you've let loose some powerful magic. You need to undo it before someone gets hurt."

"Hurt?" Hermione asked. "You don't think that was the point? This show was supposed to be mine! If someone gets hurt—" She gestured and the feather duster appeared in her hands. "—they shouldn't have gotten in my way." Snarling, she stabbed the duster at me.

At that moment, the stage lights flared bright, then plunged into darkness. Hermione gasped in surprise. I dropped low. Shimmering green fairy dust swirled above me, but I was already kicking out. My foot found Hermione's heels and, with a cry, she went down. The feather duster flew high. I rolled to my feet and snatched it out of the air.

"Next time," I told Hermione, "wear something sensible."

But I had been too slow. The lights came back up. Shrouded in a crimson cape trimmed in yellow marabou, Mitzy stood centre stage, right in the middle of the fairy circle. Her face was serene, her blond wig held high. She stood in silence, giving the audience a moment of anticipation before she began to sing.

I knew the number. I'd listened to her rehearse it many times and never had the slow, proud opening of "I Am What I Am" seemed more poignant. "Ah, Mitzy," I murmured to myself as the audience fell under the simple, earnest enchantment of her performance.

Then the song hit its stride. Mitzy's voice and the music rose together and she threw off the cape to reveal a costume of high boots, a sparkling sequin thong—and her own naked, manly chest.

The crowd went wild.

"That's right," screamed Mitzy Knish over the bridge of the song. "That's the real me—a big flaming queen and damn proud of it! You know the words. Sing it with me!"

The crowd roared its approval. At my feet, Hermione Frisson, her big moment irrevocably stolen, howled and pounded her fists against the ground.

※

In the end, I didn't even need to use the feather duster to erase the fairy circle. As Mitzy strutted across the stage, belting out her anthem, the glittering lines unravelled and drifted away in sparkling clouds, undone by the power of her pride. The crowd thought it was part of the show, but I knew better and so did Mitzy. With the magic dispersed, she got all of the other performers— even Hermione's red-assed dancers—out on the stage to sing with her. The audience met them with a thunderous ovation that completely drowned out whatever now forgotten act was playing over on the Main Stage.

The show was a triumph. Mitzy may have used up her big number early but she improvised a mash-up of "It's Not Unusual" and "Danke Schoën" with CU2 Baby Baby that left the stage littered in panties and jockstraps. I'm pretty sure that the lowly Second Stage Saturday Night Special established a record for encores that night. I know for a fact that all of the performers—including a certain pair of burlesque boys who joined Xabi for a risqué performance that nearly put the cum in come back—were immediately signed up to play the Main Stage at next year's festivities.

The only one who didn't get invited back was

Hermione Frisson, though I think the Pride organizers, unaware of her role in nearly destroying the show in the first place, would have asked her, too—if they'd been able to find her. By the time I looked away from the stage, she'd vanished. Mitzy and I went to the dressing room after the curtain finally came down, but even her costumes were gone.

The only sign that Hermione Frisson had ever been at Pride at all was a lone pasty with a long tassel that shimmered with green dust as I picked it up.

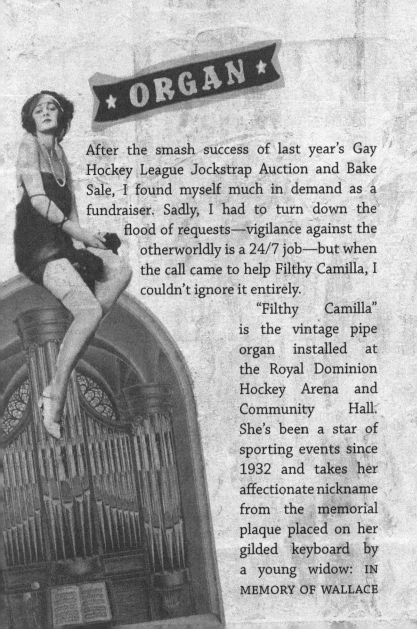

★ ORGAN ★

After the smash success of last year's Gay Hockey League Jockstrap Auction and Bake Sale, I found myself much in demand as a fundraiser. Sadly, I had to turn down the flood of requests—vigilance against the otherworldly is a 24/7 job—but when the call came to help Filthy Camilla, I couldn't ignore it entirely.

"Filthy Camilla" is the vintage pipe organ installed at the Royal Dominion Hockey Arena and Community Hall. She's been a star of sporting events since 1932 and takes her affectionate nickname from the memorial plaque placed on her gilded keyboard by a young widow: IN MEMORY OF WALLACE

VAIL, FROM CAMILLA. THE HOCKEY TEAM LOVES IT
AND SO DOES THE MILKMAN.

We're all very proud of Camilla, but she's a high
maintenance kind of girl. Her pipes need to be
cleaned regularly, her windchests have had more
reconstruction than a porn star, and the last time
her blower seized, they needed a specialist to reach
inside and jiggle things loose. I couldn't leave the
preservation society in the lurch, so I put them in
touch with the best fundraising organizers I know:
the Ladies' Senior Auxiliary of the East Sykes
United Church. The ladies have been running the
church Christmas Bazaar—not to mention the
Thanksgiving Pie Auction, the Hallelujah Summer
Day Camp, and the Easter "He is Risen" Bake-off—
for decades so I knew that the Up with Our Organ
campaign would be in good hands.

They settled on a dazzling charity casino to be held
at the arena just before Christmas when everyone
is full of good will and festive giving. It certainly
seemed like a marvellous idea to me—at least until
I walked through the door and was greeted by a pair
of young men in the costumes of Roman gladiators.

"Yo," they said in unison.

"Yo," I responded in surprise. I drew my date for
the evening aside. "Edie, what's this?"

"It's good enough for Caesar's Palace, it's good
enough for us." Edie North is a dear friend, a leading

member of the Ladies' Senior Auxiliary, and still a bona fide pussy magnet even if she's almost as old as Filthy Camilla. She was between girlfriends at the moment—the last one had recently moved to Victoria suffering from exhaustion—so she'd graciously allowed me to escort her to the casino. "Disappointed, Derby? I would have thought you'd approve."

One of the gladiators looked over his shoulder, gave me a wink, and flexed oiled muscles that made me think of roaring crowds, sun-baked arenas, and hot, dark tunnels crowded with desperate, sweaty . . . I shivered. "Oh, I approve. It's just that the theme has me a bit worried. It seems . . . off."

Edie's expression turned into a glower that would have cowed an emperor. "Dear Lord, what is it this time?" she demanded. "Zombies at the Christmas Bazaar, spirits at supper club, werewolves at Hanukkah—so help me, Derby Cavendish, I would like to have one holiday without something weird happening!"

"So would I, Edie," I said. "So would I."

A server clad in a short tunic and sandals offered us champagne. I took glasses for me and Edie, and we ventured farther into the arena. The ice surface of the Royal Dom had been covered over for the evening's event. Tuxedoes and cocktail dresses took the place of hockey sweaters, but the Roman theme of the evening had been laid on with all the subtlety of a New Jersey spray tan. Palm trees, fake columns, and reclining couches were scattered among the gambling tables, which were themselves staffed by attractive young men and women in draped togas and *stolas*. Legionaries, slaves, and gladiators of both genders—the Ladies' Senior Auxiliary can be quite progressive—moved through the room, posing for photo ops and flirting with one and all. It was sophisticated, it was decadent—and it was very, very sexual. I could see it in every drawn-out glance, every touch that lingered just a little too long. The casino had more tension than a locker room full of horned-up jocks wondering who among them would be first to pop a boner.

The ladies of the Auxiliary aren't that progressive. "I don't like this, Edie," I said. "Something is definitely wrong."

"Derby, give it a rest. There's nothing wrong." Edie drained her champagne and handed the empty flute to a passing girl in the costume of a sexy legionary—then reached out and pulled her in for a long, passionate kiss.

I gave her a few moments, then cleared my throat. Edie blinked as she realized what she was doing and quickly turned loose her prize. The girl smiled, gave her a saucy "Yo," and sauntered away. Edie looked at me. "Something is wrong, Derby."

"And I know what it is." The legionary girl's response had been the clue. Four muscular gladiators and one of the local hockey stars, apparently having been talked out of his shirt, posed for a photo nearby. "Yo!" I called to them.

"Yo!" called back all five enthusiastically. The hockey star nudged one of the gladiators and added, "Hey, buddy, that harness looks pretty hot. Could I try it on?"

I'd heard enough. "Saturnalia!" I said.

"What?" asked Edie.

"A Roman festival of frivolity and role reversal," I told her. "During Saturnalia, masters served their slaves, friends exchanged joke gifts, and chaos reigned." I swept my hand around the casino, which was becoming increasingly raucous. "It was frequently marked by gambling, as well as the traditional greeting of 'Io Saturnalia!' which is also sometimes rendered as—"

"Yo!" shouted everyone around us in unison.

"Exactly," I said. "Edie, the East Sykes Ladies' Senior Auxiliary has invoked the spirit of Saturnalia!"

"Virgin Mary on a pogo stick!" Edie cursed. "We've let loose an orgy?"

"So it would seem, which is odd because strictly speaking, orgies were more a feature of Bacchanalia, the spring festival of wine and—"

Edie punched me with a bony fist. "Never mind

that, you big whoopsie! How did this happen?"

"I don't know," I admitted.

"God in Heaven, there really is a first time for everything."

Hell hath no sarcasm like an elderly lesbian. "You're not helping, Edie. We need to figure this out before somebody does something they'll regret."

Edie winced. "Too late for that," she said as a woman's voice rose from behind me—"Dave, no one wants to see your impression of a one-armed bandit. Pull your pants up!"

I resisted the temptation to turn around. "Who had the idea to do a Roman theme for the casino?" I asked Edie. "We'll start with them."

"Them" was a sprightly little woman named Mavis Anderson whom we had to drag away from a Texas Hold'em table piled high with pieces of clothing as well as poker chips. "Damn it, Edie," Mavis said, "I almost had that young Dr. Singh down to his tiger-stripe underpants. A couple more hands and I would have shown him a pair of queens he'd never forget." She gave us a shimmy of ample bosom, for the moment still supported by an overachieving brassiere.

"Never mind him," Edie said. "Haven't you noticed things getting a little out of hand?"

"Only Dr. Singh," said Mavis with a wink.

I took her by the shoulders and forced her to

meet my gaze. "Mavis Anderson, look and see what's happening around you!"

Mavis blinked, then her eyes grew wide as she stared around the casino. A yelp of alarm escaped her, and she tried to cover herself with her hands. "What's happening?"

"Nothing that can't be fixed," I told her. "Where did you get the idea for a Roman casino? An old book? A strange dream?"

"A . . . a dream. Yes, a dream."

I knew it. "Were there instructions in this dream?" I demanded. "Rituals to be performed? What sort of otherworldly entity presented itself to you?"

Mavis's face, already flushed, turned an even deeper shade of red. "Alright, alright! It was my grandson, Braden!"

"Don't worry, Mavis," I assured her. "It may have looked like Braden in your dream, but it was something else wearing his—"

"What?" she said. "No! There was no dream. The Roman theme wasn't actually my idea. Braden suggested it."

"Mavis!" said Edie.

"I wanted to do a nice winter wonderland theme!" Mavis protested. "Braden said it would be more fun to do sexy Romans like those hunky boys they have handing out condoms at the Pride parade. And I thought, why not? Most of the volunteers are

Braden's friends from the frats and sororities at the university. A lot of them even had their own togas."

"Bedsheets, Mavis! They had their own bedsheets!"

"Alright," I sighed. "Where's Braden now?"

"In the community hall. They're supposed to be getting ready for a big dance number."

"I bet they are," I said. "Come on, Edie."

A side door connected the arena to the community hall, but the crowd became ever more unruly as we pushed toward it. I spotted the minister of East Sykes United double-fisting champagne while our local city councillor ground against him like he was a stripper pole. The gaming tables were largely forgotten or utterly subverted: the roulette layout was covered in shots instead of chips, genitals had been drawn on the Big Six wheel, and when someone at the craps table yelled "Kiss them for luck!" they weren't talking about dice. Only Edie's well-placed elbows and knees kept us moving forward.

"Nicely done!" I gasped as we finally broke free.

"You don't spend three years following Lilith Fair without slogging through a few mud pits," she said. "The smell of dirt in the rain still makes me horny." She pushed aside the shirtless hockey star where he was making out with two of the gladiators, and I threw open the door to the community hall.

"I'm looking for Braden Anderson!" I shouted.

There was no response—for good reason. As I'd expected, the frat boys and sorority girls gathered in the hall were well past worrying about their big dance number. Lacking the long-standing shame and pent-up lust of their elders, they'd apparently skipped the preliminary craziness taking over the casino floor and gotten right to the orgy. The warm air in the community hall smelled of sweat, sex, and floor polish as knots of nearly naked forms slid together in languid sensuality. For a moment, I wondered if Edie and I were doing the right thing. When it came down to it, everyone seemed to be enjoying themselves and surely it would just be rude to interrupt. . . .

Edie poked me sharply. "Quit staring, you pervert!"

"I wasn't staring, I was assessing the situation," I told her. "You can't rush these things."

But Edie had a point—we didn't have all night. And while it was one thing to let people get their freak on of their own free will, what was happening at the Royal Dom was not natural. Being careful not to step on anyone, I ventured through the door and called again, "I'm looking for Braden Anderson." Nothing. I tried once more. "Is there a Braden here?"

A young man groaned with frustration and separated himself from his partners. "I'm Braden. Braden Vail."

His hair was copper-red and dishevelled, his face flushed with arousal. The toga he wore might once have been carefully wrapped, but the evening's exertions had left it hanging as loose as the hinges on a bathhouse door—except below the waist, where it stood out in a tent big enough to entertain a circus. Even Edie let out a low whistle of amazement.

I wrenched my gaze up to his face and tried to think about Margaret Thatcher in leather gear. "Are you Mavis Anderson's grandson?" I asked.

He rolled his eyes, which was answer enough for me. "What's she done now? I'm kind of in the middle of something."

"You're in the middle of it, alright!" I told him. "What made you suggest a Roman theme to your grandmother?"

Braden shrugged. "Caesar's Palace, man."

"That's what I said," commented Edie.

"Still not helping." I looked back to Braden. This wasn't adding up. I could see in his eyes that he didn't have the arcane knowledge necessary to manipulate people on this scale. And as I'd pointed out to Edie, this was Saturnalia, not Bacchanalia. A festival of freedom and role reversal, but not orgies. "There must be something else," I said.

"It's just a big toga party," said Braden, adjusting his costume with the effect of revealing even more sweat-streaked skin. Margaret Thatcher in leather, I thought desperately. Winston Churchill in bondage. Braden just shrugged again. "Everybody loves it."

Suddenly I had the answer, unlocked by those three little words. "Everybody loves it," I repeated. "This isn't about Saturnalia at all." I pointed at Braden. "You've roused the spirit of Filthy Camilla!"

"What the hell are you talking about?" he demanded. "Yeah, Camilla Vail was my great-grandmother on my father's side—you don't think we're reminded of that every time we watch a hockey game? You think I've done something? You think she needs any more disrespect?"

"Not at all. And I don't think you've done anything deliberately, but Saturnalia is a date of power. Camilla's descendant fulfilling the Saturnalia ritual of gambling on holy ground? You've definitely roused something."

"Holy ground?" asked Edie. "Derby, it's a hockey arena."

"And I guarantee it's seen more prayers than East Sykes United." I grabbed her with one hand and Braden—John A. MacDonald in a gimp suit, I told myself—with the other. "If I'm right, we'll find the answer with Filthy Camilla herself!"

The organ console was upstairs in a booth overlooking the ice surface. Before we'd even reached the top of the stairs, I knew my hunch had been correct. There was a tension in the air. When I opened the door to the booth, that tension exploded with a pressure that made us stagger.

Inside, the gaudy gilt and ivory of the keyboards shimmered and it seemed to me that I could hear the swelling, full-throated music of the pipes. A woman stood by the console, shimmering like the organ. She wore a dress from the 1930s and her hair was copper-gold; it was clear that Braden got his looks from his great-grandmother. Desire rolled off of her in waves, eighty years of sexual craving finally finding a release. With each wave of lust, the sounds of depravity from the casino below built in volume.

"Oh, shit," said Braden.

I stepped forward, raising a hand. "Camilla Vail, you must stop this! I command you!"

The phantom pipe music rose. Camilla just smiled and caressed her breasts, then spread her arms in loving invitation.

A chill of horror spread through me. I felt my testicles signal full retreat. Surely she didn't . . . "Oh, shit," I said and froze.

But Edie pulled me back. "Hold my purse, Derby," she said, "I've got this." She slapped her clutch into my hands and I realized there was a gleam in her eye. Camilla's smile faltered for a moment, then she raised an eyebrow and the smile came back.

Before I could stop her, Edie had stepped through the door. The last thing I heard before it slammed in my face was her husky greeting of "Yo."

※

I'd like to say that the fundraiser was a success. Perhaps in the end it was: the Up with Our Organ campaign was fully funded, though I'm sure it was more through guilt and hush money than anything else. The police chief—who I last saw crawling under the roulette wheel with a bottle of vodka and one of the slave girls—promised a thorough investigation into what was clearly a mass roofie-ing, but that promise just faded into obscurity. The board of directors of the Royal Dominion Arena quietly passed a motion prohibiting gambling in the building, and the East Sykes Ladies' Senior Auxiliary banned charity casinos from their fundraising repertoire. Even bingo attendance in the city plummeted for a time, and while it eventually recovered, no one giggles at O69 anymore.

And we owed it all to Edie's sacrifice. Within moments of the door to the organ booth closing behind her, I felt the tension in the air ease. Braden and I waited, though, and only when the sounds of Saturnalia chaos gave way to awkward silence— as well as the occasional exclamations of "Kathy, how could you?" or "But I was wearing pants when I walked in!" and "Madam, kindly remove your tongue"—did we break down the door and go after her.

I found Edie lying underneath Filthy Camilla, her dress hiked up around her thighs and a satisfied smile on her face. She looked so peaceful and content that I almost couldn't bring myself to disturb her. Fortunately, I didn't have to.

"Quit staring," she said without opening her eyes.

"I'm not staring," I told her.

"You're checking out my cooch."

"Trust me, Edie. I'm not." I held up my jacket while she rearranged her dress, then Braden and I helped her to her feet. "So," I asked, "how was it?"

"I'm buying myself season tickets for Christmas," she said.

"Oh? You're into hockey now?"

"Hockey? No." Edie trailed her fingers fondly across Camilla's keyboard. "But I'm a big fan of the organ."

"It has to be just right," said my friend Matthew Plumper. "Big, but not too big. Long and smooth and glossy. And the thicker, the better."

"Matthew," I said, "please just pick one. It's only a Christmas tree."

"Only a Christmas tree?" Matthew paused in the snow and gave me a haughty look. His breath steamed in the wintery air. "My, my. Is Derby Cavendish getting testy? Does Derby Cavendish not like the cold?"

"Derby Cavendish," I told him, "sees nothing wrong with getting his Christmas tree like decent, normal people: from a parking lot or a grocery store, not some—" I gestured around us. "—forsaken wilderness."

To be fair, the forsaken wilderness in question was the famous Wood Family Christmas Tree Farm, well-known for their seasonal sleigh rides, roaming carol singers, plentiful hot chocolate dispensers, and vintage advertising featuring such classic slogans as WOOD CHRISTMAS TREES: WAKE UP WITH WOOD ON CHRISTMAS. Matthew has been dragging me along on his annual excursion into the winter countryside for many years, but it never gets easier. I'm a city boy by heart, and I'd rather be toasting my buns by a fire than chilling them in the snow. As far as I'm concerned, the only proper place for ice is in a cocktail.

But that wasn't the only reason I was on edge this year. Like people who leave their shopping until Christmas Eve, Matthew waits until the last minute to get his Christmas tree and this year he'd left it even later than usual. Christmas was only four days away and that meant we were outdoors in the countryside on December 21: the eve of the Winter Solstice, the longest night of the year, and one of the most dangerous of the ancient dates of power.

And Matthew was dithering over a Christmas tree.

I glanced at the late afternoon sun as it dipped toward the horizon. "They had some very nice trees ready to go beside the front gate," I reminded him. "Firs as thick as the bush on a '70s porn star."

"It's not the same," Matthew said as he wandered deeper into the winter wonderland. "Unless you chop them down yourself, they've just been sitting and getting stale. Like I always say, everything is better uncut."

I sighed and paused long enough to top up my rapidly cooling hot chocolate from the whisky flask—don't go Christmas shopping without one!— that I kept in my pocket. As I returned the flask to its hiding place though, I noticed a strange stillness had fallen over the tree farm. The jingle of sleigh bells seemed suddenly distant. The off-key songs of the carollers were as faint as their hopes for a musical career and getting fainter.

"Matthew," I said, "something is wrong."

"Oh, Derby, calm down. There's nothing here to worry about." Even as Matthew spoke, however, his voice grew muffled. I couldn't see him anymore— the thick branches of Wood's famous trees had swallowed him up. I started after him, but then I heard a silvery tinkling laugh that froze my already cold blood. I knew that laugh. I whirled around.

Standing in the pale light of the setting sun were four teenage girls. One of them was a willowy redhead with eyes like glowing embers. She hissed like a snake. One of them had black hair and green eyes. She growled. The third was pale as brittle, age-yellowed linen. She was silent but she grinned at me with sharp teeth in black gums.

The fourth was my nemesis. "Hello, Bethany," I said.

"Derby—it's been so long. I'd say you're looking well, but it looks more like you've been hitting the weekend buffet seven days a week." She smoothed the front of her puffy pink vest. "Notice anything different?"

Bethany may look like a high school cheerleader, but she's everything dark and evil with lip gloss and white yoga pants. If she was around, something was definitely wrong. "Well, the last time I saw you, you were a stain on a barroom floor, so there's that," I said. I squinted at her. "Are your boobs finally coming in?"

Bethany's face darkened. The pale girl with sharp teeth made a dry rasping sound like something long dead trying to laugh. Bethany shot her a nasty look. "Cleo!" she snapped and the girl fell silent. Bethany turned to me again. "Take a closer look, Derby," she snarled. "Take a real close look."

I didn't need to. The moment I'd glanced at her, I'd seen the amulet she wore around her neck. Worked in iron and silver, it showed the kind of rectangular maze pattern found on certain Bronze Age vault barrows, ancient tombs with doors through which sunlight shone only once a year—when the sun died on the winter solstice and passed the long night in the underworld.

My mouth went dry. "What do you want, Bethany?"

"What do I ever want, Derby?" she said. "Your meddling do-good ass in a box six feet underground!" She snapped her fingers and pointed at me. "Girls, go get him!"

I threw my hot chocolate at her.

It wasn't remotely hot enough anymore to hurt her, but as the sticky brown mess splattered over her white pants and pink vest, Bethany wailed like a siren. "That's going to stain like a motherfucker, you bitch!"

But I was already turning and charging into the trees where Matthew had gone. "Matthew!" I shouted. "Matthew! Run! Bethany's here!"

From somewhere not too far away, I thought I heard Matthew curse. I followed the sound and Matthew's footprints, but before I'd run thirty feet, a vast roaring rose around me and a howling surge of wind knocked me flat. Snow and loose pine needles stung my skin. Battered by the wind, I tumbled across the ground before slamming hard into something very solid. The wind died away as suddenly as it had risen and I found myself staring up into another of the tree farm's friendly ads— WOOD CHRISTMAS TREES: GET WOOD FOR YOUR FAMILY. I hauled myself upright and looked around.

The wind had scoured away any trace of Matthew's passing. I called his name again and again, but there wasn't even the hint of a response. The long rows of trees were more silent now than before. And, I realized, significantly darker. I turned around and found the sun just in time to watch the last of its red disc slip below the horizon. In that moment, all of the heat and light seemed to go out of the world, leaving only cold moonglow behind. The true winter solstice had begun.

I heard Bethany's laugh again. I looked up to find her floating among the tree branches. There was no sign of her three harpies. "Where's Matthew?" I demanded.

"Safe at the farm gate, I imagine," she said. "He was gone before we even started talking—I don't give a shit about him. This is all about you, Derby."

"You don't think I'll find my way out?"

Bethany smiled, her teeth flashing in the thin light, and touched the amulet around her neck. There was another rushing roar as wind shook the trees—except that I felt nothing. With an ass-puckering chill as cold as a rim job from a snowman, I realized that the movement wasn't wind at all, but the trees rearranging themselves. In an instant, I was surrounded by thick, green walls. Here and there I could see openings among the trees, but I knew in my gut that any passage wouldn't lead far. Wood Family Tree Farm had become a labyrinth just like the one on Bethany's amulet.

I glared up at the teenage witch. "I suppose your

girls are waiting to hunt me through the maze?"

"Oh hell, no," said Bethany. "We're going somewhere cozy with popcorn and watching *Love Actually*." Her smile got a little wider. "You're going to have a very long, very cold night, Derby."

I snorted and felt in my pocket. Like a Boy Scout, I'm always prepared, and my whisky flask wasn't the only useful thing I had on me. "We're in the woods, Bethany." I held up the lighter that I carry. "I can make a nice toasty fire to last the night."

Bethany only yawned. A nagging doubt took root in my stomach. I looked at the lighter in my hand, then flipped it open and flicked the wheel a few times.

Nothing happened.

"The long nights of winter terrified the ancients," said Bethany. Her voice took on a rolling, hollow tone as if she spoke with the weight of ages. "As the season turned colder and died, even the sun grew weak. Nights became longer and darker until surely it seemed that the sun would never return again. It had passed for the last time into the west where all dead things go. In the underworld, the wolves of legend would devour it and all of the fires of the world would go out. Forever."

She looked at me with dark and empty eyes— then laughed her tinkling laugh again. "So good night, Derby Cavendish. Sleep tight, don't let the bedbugs bite!"

"Bethany," I said, "you are a stone-cold cunt."

"You say the sweetest things." She smiled again. "You know, I hate mixing mythologies, but if you really feel like being hunted through a maze . . ."

I felt a subtle shift in the air. Hidden by the trees, something bellowed like a bull justifiably angry at being pulled from someplace warm into a chilly death trap. "A minotaur?" I asked Bethany. "Not very original."

"Sometimes you have to go with the classics." She blew me a kiss. "I'll check on your corpse in the morning."

Then she was gone and I was alone in the night. Well, not entirely alone. The snuffling and grunting of the half-man, half-bull was getting closer. Standing still wasn't going to do me any good. I turned and plunged deeper into the tree maze, thinking desperately. I was never going to outrun a minotaur in a labyrinth, and even if I did, I'd certainly freeze before morning. Bethany had chosen a perfect time to strike: the primeval magic of the winter solstice, all but forgotten in the modern world, was more powerful than anything I could invoke to defeat it.

And yet those winter-fearing ancients of long ago had survived. They might have had fire, but what had they done when the fire died?

A sudden bellow from the minotaur as he caught my scent startled me. I looked back for a moment—

and the answer hit me in the face. Or rather across the chest. One moment I was running and the next I was on the ground, staring up at the wayward fir branch that had laid me out like a stripper ready for body shots. Snow drifted into my face from the thick-clustered needles and I laughed.

"Christmas trees!" I crowed. "Christmas trees!"

I had a plan, but I'd still need help. Fortunately, Bethany had given me the means to save myself. I jumped back to my feet and raced on, searching for the last thing I needed to make my plan come together. I found it in a little clearing among the paths of the maze and not a moment too soon. The minotaur's thundering footfalls were close. I could hear the huffing of his breath. I whipped off my jacket—soaked in sweat in spite of the plummeting temperature—held it out like a matador's cape, and spun around to face my pursuer just as he appeared.

I very nearly surrendered right there. As with most otherworldly creatures, a natural glamour concealed the minotaur's true form. In this case, a stunningly gorgeous glamour with massive, meaty muscles and a neck thicker than my leg. He looked like a bodybuilder—in fact, he probably was a bodybuilder, snatched away by Bethany's spell in the middle of a workout if the rag of a tank top and the sweat shorts he wore were anything to go by. Of course, I know enough to see past the glamour of the otherworldly. Even so, with heavy horns, coarse black chest hair, and strong, only slightly bovine features, he was one hell of a good-looking man-bull. And me without my cowboy hat or chaps!

But his eyes, when he fixed them on me, had the tell-tale red glow of compulsion. I stood my ground, jacket raised tauntingly. The minotaur let out a final bellow, lowered those impressive horns, and charged.

At the last moment, I whipped my jacket away and threw myself aside. The minotaur, unable to stop himself, crashed head first into the obstacle I had been hiding: another of the tree farm's very solid advertising signs. WOOD CHRISTMAS TREES: NOTHING ELSE SMELLS LIKE WOOD.

As the minotaur staggered back, momentarily stunned, I jumped in and slapped my hand on his head. "From chains and bonds of all kinds, I release you!" I declared. "Your body and mind be free!"

The minotaur groaned and snorted, then looked at me with clear, if confused, eyes. I quickly took charge and described our situation, pointing out that if we didn't work together, we'd both be frozen solid by morning. The minotaur nodded—slowly. I smiled to put him at ease and introduced myself. "I'm Derby," I said.

"They call me Horse."

It was an odd nickname for a half-bull, but I wasn't going to argue. "Horse, I need you to pull down as many Christmas tree branches as you can. We're going to make ourselves a little den and huddle together for the night." His eyebrows rose. "For warmth," I clarified. "Sharing body heat."

His eyes stayed on mine. I became aware that my sweaty clothes were becoming stiff—with ice— while frost had crept across both Horse's hairy skin and his skimpy workout gear.

"We should probably," I added, "take these wet clothes off, too."

Horse gave me a slow smile, hooked his thumbs into the waistband of his shorts, and pushed them down. Suddenly I understood his nickname. I swallowed and pulled out my flask. "Whisky?" I asked.

※

By the time Bethany showed up the next morning, I had a lovely little fire going and moisture was steaming off my clothes. The sun had, of course, risen after the solstice. Fire had returned to the world, and the trees of the farm had shifted back to their proper orderly rows. Bethany didn't look at all happy to see me alive, warm, and maybe even with a certain, satisfied glow. Her face screwed up until it looked like she was going to swallow herself. "How are you still alive?"

"Christmas trees," I said. I patted the remains of the cozy nest that Horse and I had made for ourselves. "Evergreens, to be precise: a symbol of life in the middle of winter and a powerful counter to the magic of the solstice. You screwed up, Bethany."

"Fuck you, Derby," said Bethany. Her eyes narrowed. "Where's my minotaur?"

Right on cue, Horse exploded from under the snow and tree branches with a roar and grabbed for her. Bethany shrieked and vanished like inhibitions after tequila. Horse looked disappointed but I rubbed his broad, snow-dusted shoulders.

"Don't worry," I said. "She'll be back. She always comes back."

"Derby! Derby!" Matthew's voice cut through the morning. I returned his call and he came running out of the woods. "Derby, what happened? Where were you? I tried coming back last night, but it was so cold and dark—"

He stopped short as he saw Horse and his brow furrowed in confusion. "Don't worry, Matthew," I told him. "Bethany's gone and we're all fine."

"But it was such a long night."

"Oh, Matthew," I said with a smile and a sideways look at Horse. "The *longest*."

I first encountered the otherworldly at an early age. I was seven and it was the night before St. Patrick's Day. I was wide awake, worrying about what I'd wear—green is not my colour—when I heard my closet door open. I've never been afraid of anything in my closet, so naturally I sat up in bed to see what it was. The moonlight was streaming through my bedroom window, and I found myself face to face with a strange spidery thing that was all long legs and glowing eyes.

I won't lie: I came close to peeing myself.

But I held it together, stared down that monster, and demanded "So what do *you* want?"

The spider thing shuddered and folded in on itself as if in confusion at finding me awake, then answered with a rattling, drawn-out voice, "I'm here for your niiightmaaares."

"You want a nightmare?" I said. "What do I wear to school tomorrow?"

It squinted at me with its multitude of eyes. "Blaaack—with one green accessory."

I was surprised I hadn't thought of that myself, but then it was advanced fashion for a seven-year-old. "Thank you," I said.

"Dooon't mention it," said the spider. "Must be going. Many less-confident children to terrify." It squeezed into the closet again but looked back at me before it closed the door. "You're an unusual chiiild, Derby Cavendish."

"Flatterer!" I called after it, but the spider was gone. I slept well, and the next day my shamrock goth look was the hit of the playground. The spider's visit had roused my curiosity however, and I began what would become my ongoing research into the supernatural and otherworldly. I already had a gut feeling that the next time I encountered such a being, I would need to be ready. And I was right; when a hellhound came howling at a group of trick-or-treaters the following Halloween, I stood my ground and tossed it candy from my little pumpkin bucket. The devil dog gobbled it down and whined for more. So I fed it and fed it until my bucket was empty and that greedy hellhound was full of treats. Sugary, sugary treats. Have you ever dropped a marshmallow into a campfire and watched it puff up into a searing, sticky mess? The stain that hellhound left on the sidewalk warned the otherworldly off of our neighbourhood for years afterward.

I learned three things very quickly. First, that the creatures and forces of the otherworldly, both kindly and malevolent, were for some reason drawn to me. Second, that these visitations took place most frequently, though not exclusively, on dates of mystical and mythical power: Halloween and Hanukkah, solstices, equinoxes, Elvis Presley's birthday, and so on.

And third, that I would need to study the

otherworldly for my own protection—and the protection of those around me. I was, as that spider had seen, unusual. Anyone can see the otherworldly, but most people's minds simply refuse to acknowledge the existence of anything unnatural even when it's right in front of them. The other trick-or-treaters, the ones who ran, remembered the hellhound only as a loose dog. The adults who went looking for it later saw the ashes only as the remnants of a bag of candy set on fire. Of course, you can imagine who got blamed for that! It takes someone unusual, someone open to the strange, to see what's really happening. I knew that I could—nay, had to—make a difference. I resolved to stand up to the otherworldly in any situation, no matter how dangerous, unpleasant, or unexpected. In fact, over the years I've become rather accustomed to the unexpected.

Of course, I don't think anyone ever really expects the end of the world.

1. NEW YEAR'S EVE

The street outside the Lumber Yard, the city's most popular gay bar, was packed tight. Tighter than a go-go boy's thong. Tighter than the closet at a political convention. Tighter than a virgin ass on double penetration night at the bathhouse. Tighter than—well, you get the picture. New Year's Eve is a big deal in the gay village. Pride may be more heavily attended, Halloween may be stranger, and the Spring Garden Street Show more inexplicably anticipated, but New Year's is an excuse to party in the middle of winter. And this year the celebration was even bigger because the Lumber Yard was taking the party outside. They'd obtained an outdoor liquor licence and set up a massive street party, complete with temporary bars, patio heaters, and a long stage built out from their famous panoramic windows. Simply everyone had come down to the village for the show.

And it was all because of my good friend, rising drag star Aaron Silverman—better known as Miss Mitzy Knish, the original Hebrew Hot Pocket. From drag night appearances at bars like the Lumber Yard and Squeal, to such acclaimed solo shows as "Sausage Party" and "Titanic II: Just the Tip (of the Iceberg)," to spectacular main stage performances at Pride festivals around the country, Mitzy was on top of the world and riding it hard. Now she was poised to shoot into her next big project: an actual television series! Tentatively titled either *Mitzy's Big Year* or *The Drag Queen's Guide to the Holidays*—or, as the lower brow of our friends have suggested, *Have Tuck, Will Travel*—the show would see Mitzy in a fabulous year-long tour exploring various holidays around the country.

How better to kick off production than on New Year's Eve in Mitzy's hometown, surrounded by her biggest fans? Somewhere out in the seething mass of people in front of the Lumber Yard, Mitzy and her camera crew circulated, pumping up the crowd, pimping out the show, and giving away noisemakers and vodka shots with reckless abandon. After all, a noisy and well-lubricated crowd is a happy crowd.

Personally, I was sticking by one of the bars while Mitzy did her thing. It was somewhere between eleven and eleven-thirty, and I'd been on the go since noon. Aaron had called in a panic, begging me to come out with him for moral support. I knew he didn't need it—whether in sneakers or stilettos, Aaron is a consummate performer—but I'd agreed because he's my friend. I'd spent the afternoon watching as the camera crew shot B-roll of Aaron doing sound checks on the still-under-construction stage and picking out his costumes (never mind that they'd all been carefully selected weeks ago). I'd spent the early evening lingering in the background while the crew, by now as thoroughly enamoured as any fan, filmed Aaron's transformation into Mitzy. I'd spent the mid- to late-evening following along in Mitzy's wake as she dropped in on various New Year's parties around the city, from a sedate dinner party of seniors, to a chaotic play-date party for children and their exhausted parents, to a raucous university house party that the police shut down just as we pulled away.

Now, as midnight and Mitzy's big number approached, it was time to catch my breath. I drained the last of my drink and gestured to the bartender. "Another, please."

"What will it be?"

The bartender who stood across from me wasn't the same bartender as before—and I can't say I was entirely disappointed. He was a handsome man with a long, sharp nose and thick, curly black hair and beard. "Vodka and tonic," I said. I watched him while he made the drink. There was something slightly odd about him, something that I couldn't immediately place. I cleared my mind and focused my gaze, looking at him with the second sight.

The glamour of the otherworldly fell away. Tall, furry ears like a donkey's poked up through my bartender's curly hair. When he turned, I saw that his pants had been split at the back to accommodate a long, drooping tail. My bartender winked and swished his tail playfully as he set my drink in front of me. "Admiring my ass, Derby?" he asked.

I blinked in surprise, and the long ears and tail vanished. My instincts, however, remained atingle. Not all otherworldly beings are malicious and I try to treat them all fairly, but it was a mistake to trust any of them on first sight. "You know me?"

"Word gets around. You're something of a legend."

"I have my moments," I said modestly.

The bartender offered me his hand. "Tarik."

"You're a satyr."

"I know—a satyr working as a bartender. Shocker." Tarik smiled. "It was a natural fit. Well, that or porn."

In ancient Greece and Anatolia, satyrs were the companions of Dionysus, god of wine and fertility. If you're picturing horny, hairy-legged goat men, stop it. Those are fauns and they're Roman; satyrs come from further east and are considerably classier. Dionysus and most of the other old gods have fallen on hard times in the modern world, but satyrs might have been custom made for it. They're legendary for their ability to mix a drink and notorious for their unflagging libido—in addition to having the ears and tails of asses, satyrs are ithyphallic. Contrary to what you may think, that doesn't mean "fishdicked." It's the polite way of saying satyrs get more wood than a horny lumberjack.

I was strongly tempted to check for myself, but I kept my eyes on his handsome, handsome face. "I haven't seen you at the Lumber Yard before," I said.

"I just got hired. I haven't been in town long." Tarik glanced down the length of the bar, then produced two shot glasses and filled them with tequila. "Join me? On the house."

I hesitated. One of the first rules in dealing with any type of otherworldly is never accept food or drink. On the other hand, we were at a public bar, the tequila came from a common bottle, and Tarik's eyes had a certain sparkle to them that was making more than my instincts tingle. It was New Year's Eve, after all—why not see where this went? I picked up a shot glass and clinked it against Tarik's. "To the new year."

He met and held my gaze. "To you, Derby," he said and my tingle turned into a slow burn. Our eyes stayed locked as we tossed back the shots. Tarik leaned across the bar—

"Derby! Derby!"

Mitzy came crashing through the crowd, completely destroying what would potentially have been one of the hottest kisses of my life. Tarik smiled again and drew back. I suppressed a groan and turned to Mitzy. She looked as fabulous as ever, but her eyes were wide with panic. My frustration fell away instantly. "What's wrong?"

Mitzy was holding something close to her body. She opened her arms just enough to show me a small monkey huddled up against her ample, if artificial, bosom. "This!"

I raised an eyebrow. "Where did you get the monkey, Mitz?" I looked behind her. "Did you ditch your camera man?"

"This *is* my camera man!" She held out the trembling monkey. "One minute I'm mugging, the next I'm playing Jane with Cheetah trying to climb into my tits."

"No one saw anything?"

"Of course not!" She noticed Tarik staring at us and stiffened. "I mean, that is . . ."

All good drag queens are more than they seem. In Mitzy's case, she's more and then some. "It's okay," I said. "He's otherworldly, too. Tarik, Mitzy Knish; Mitzy, Tarik."

"Drink?" asked Tarik.

"God, yes." Mitzy handed the monkey off to me and grabbed the shot Tarik poured for her, throwing it down like she was bailing a sinking boat. Meanwhile, I held the monkey out at arm's length and studied it closely. The animal was shaking and its eyes were darting everywhere, signs that there was a terrified human mind inside the simian skull.

"It's a transformation," I said. "A real monkey would probably be screaming and fighting to run."

"But why, Derby?" demanded Mitzy. "Why would someone do this? Who would do this?"

I focused my second sight on the monkey, looking past the veil of the glamour. As I expected, I could see a human form, twisted and compressed, behind the monkey shape. The fine coat of shimmering powder as green as poison that clung to the creature's fur was not something I'd expected, however. "Fairy dust," I said. "This is fairy magic."

Mitzy's mouth tightened into a plump little pucker. "Hermione Frisson," she growled—rather literally and with enough force to make Tarik step back a pace.

"Easy!" I said quickly. Mitzy's secret is that she's very likely the world's only Jewish drag queen werewolf, the result of a quick nip at summer camp when Aaron was just a boy still playing with his mother's heels. Fortunately, Mitzy is in full control of the wolf most of the time. There are a few things, however, that can still bring out the beast in her, and it looked like we were facing one of them.

But Mitzy took a deep breath and nodded. "I'm fine." She peeled back her lips. "Teeth?"

"No fangs, just a little lipstick."

As she cursed and scrubbed away the cherry-red stain, Tarik leaned closer again. "This Hermione Frisson is a fairy?"

I could understand his confusion. Fairies are among the rarest and most reclusive of the otherworldly. "No," I told him, "Hermione is human, but somehow she's learned fairy magic. Unfortunately, she's taken a sharp dislike to Mitzy. A couple of years ago, she was the hottest burlesque star in the city—until she tried using a fairy circle to sabotage a show Mitzy was in."

"And you can bet she blames me for it," said Mitzy. "Now she's trying to wreck my show in revenge!" She squeezed her hands into fists. Her knuckles cracked.

"Nails!" I reminded her. She flinched and spread her fingers to inspect them.

"Still good. What are we going to do, Derby? I need my camera man back!"

"Don't worry." I looked to Tarik. "Do you have any salt to go with that tequila?"

He darted down the bar and brought back a half-full salt shaker and bowl of lime wedges. "Thoughtful," I said, "but all I need is the salt." I set the monkey on the counter, then took the top off the shaker and poured a small pile into my hand. "Fairy magic is tricky. It's almost always tied to dusk, midnight, or dawn, but in different ways. Some spells break at those times. Others become permanent. It's hard to know. So it's safest to break the spell early. Fortunately, that's generally not too hard."

I looked around to make sure no one was paying undue attention. The glamour of the otherworldly would hide what was about to happen, but there was no sense taking chances. The glamour could only be stretched so far. "Be undone!" I commanded and flicked the salt at the monkey. The animal screeched, there was a sharp flash of green light—

—and Mitzy's camera man was sitting on the edge of the bar, looking confused but none the worse for time spent a few rungs down the evolutionary ladder. He even still had his camera with him. Mitzy, quick to react, took his hand and pulled him to his feet. "Are you okay, Jim? You were looking unsteady for a minute. All good? Let's find the others and get backstage. It's almost time for the big number."

She pushed him away into the crowd, then looked over her shoulder at me. "Find Hermione and stop her!"

"Count on it!"

"Can I help?" Tarik asked. "What does she look like?"

"A tall, leggy brunette with a fake French accent," I told him. "At least she was the last time I saw her. She could look like anyone now—fairy magic is all about charms, illusions, and transformations. Even without magic, Hermione's costumes are impeccable. Credit where credit is due, the woman is amazing. But she is dangerous. You're better off staying here."

"I can keep an eye open for her at least and call you if I see her. Give me your number." A slow smile spread across his lips. A matching fire settled in between my navel and knees.

Before I could say anything, however, a shout of alarm and outrage rose from within the crowd— followed a moment later by a plaintive howl and a surge of frightened bodies. The fire turned as cold as lube from the fridge. I forgot my sexy satyr bartender in an instant and went to the aid of my friend.

※

In spite of my fears, I found Mitzy unharmed and untransformed on the very steps of the Lumber Yard. Her camera man was still himself as well, and even the crowd was settling down a bit. Mitzy caught my eye, however, and pointed at the source of the howl, which had now subsided to an uneasy whimpering. Surrounded by concerned dog lovers, a lovely black Labrador retriever crouched trembling on the pavement. A glance with the second sight confirmed that the animal was a man transformed. Hermione had struck again!

I swiftly claimed the dog as my own dear pet who had gotten away from me in the chaos of the crowd and the well-meaning citizens dispersed. The instant they had their backs turned, I threw a handful of salt at the dog. Once again, there was a green flash—and the dog became a dazed man. I helped him to stand. "Easy there, you'll feel better in a minute. Let's get you and Mitzy inside so the show can start."

"Inside?" He blinked. "But all my friends are out here."

"Derby—" Mitzy had come down the stairs. She caught my arm and pulled me away from the confused man to whisper in my ear. "He's not part of my crew. I don't know who he is!"

"What?"

"I was going inside and I saw him transform right beside me. He's just some random guy."

"That doesn't make any sense." I looked back at the man, already staggering away, who I'd saved. "Why would Hermione attack a stranger? Maybe she thought he was with you."

"We've got to stop her, Derby! Even if no one notices it, I can't go on with a nutbar throwing magic around. Somebody could get hurt."

"I'll take care of it," I told her firmly. "You get out on that stage and don't stop, no matter what happens. *Mitzy's Big Year* is just getting started." I pushed her toward the door of the Lumber Yard. The show's production manager was already standing there, tapping urgently at her watch. Mitzy took a deep breath, lifted her head high, and walked up the stairs like a star.

I waited on edge, alert for another attack, until she was through the door. Unless Hermione had managed to slip inside the bar—and I was almost certain she was instead still lurking in the crowd outside—Mitzy was safe until she re-emerged on the stage for her opening number and the big countdown to midnight. That gave me a very short window to find Hermione and put an end to her mischief. And find her, I swore to myself, I would. Nobody was going to mess with my friend's shining moment.

I stood on the steps to scan the crowd with both normal and second sight. Nothing seemed out of the ordinary. Everyone was laughing, eager for the show to start. Everyone was beautiful, dressed to the sixes and nines for New Year's Eve. I cursed and waded directly into the crowd. Hermione had to be nearby. The kind of magic she was working required the caster to be close to the victim—the closer, the better.

"Where are you, Hermione Frisson?" I muttered to myself.

"Why, I am here," said a breathy voice with an accent like Gauloises and croissants. "I'm right behind you, Derby Cavendish."

I whirled around. She was there—or rather, *he* was. No wonder I hadn't been able to spot Hermione. Dressed in a slim-fitting tuxedo and a simple white silk scarf, her breasts bound flat and her hair slicked down, she made an exquisite, if androgynous, man. I must have looked past her half a dozen times without realizing who I was seeing. Now she pursed her lips into a mocking rosebud and slid a hand down her lapel. "Beautiful, isn't it? I realized that if that hairy crossdresser could make himself a woman, I could make myself a man."

"It fooled me," I said coldly. "What are you up to, Hermione?"

She ignored me. "I may even make it part of my act. I will call him Hermes. It would only be appropriate. Mitzy Knish stole my spotlight. Now I will steal hers—*and you won't stop me!*"

The hand on her lapel flicked like a striking snake. I caught a glimpse of green fairy dust—

—then I was among a forest of legs and looking up, way up, at Hermione's pretty man-face. I sat down in surprise and caught a tail beneath my hindquarters. My arms and hands had become white-furred forelegs and paws. I could see whiskers in the periphery of my vision.

I was a cat. A white cat.

I'd been so focused on the danger to Mitzy that I hadn't considered my own danger. "Damn it!" I spat.

The words came out as a hiss, but apparently Hermione had no trouble understanding me. "Oh, poor Derby. Finally outsmarted." She reached down with hands bigger than my head and picked me up. Still a little dazed from my sudden change in perspective, I didn't resist. Hermione held me in front of her face and considered me with narrowed eyes. "Now why did the spell work properly on you, but not on that dick in a dress?"

It took me a second to realize who she was talking about—and another to realize what that meant. "You were trying to cast your spell on *Mitzy*!"

Hermione laughed at my cat screeches. "Of course I was. You think I wanted to transform those other two nobodies? What a waste! Who would have missed them? But if Mitzy Knish suddenly couldn't be found just minutes before her big moment, what then? The show must go on—and look, here is Hermione Frisson, a real star and a real woman, ready to perform."

So there was her plan. "You're insane," I said—or rather, meowed. "It would never work."

The rosebud lips pressed into a hard line. "Perhaps not, but I would at least have destroyed Mitzy, yes? And thanks to you, I still have one more chance to do that. Mitzy is going to disappear before her fans' very eyes!"

As if on cue, the stage lights came up. A roar of anticipation rose from the crowd. Mitzy's show was about to begin.

"Get comfortable, Derby," said Hermione. "You're

going to have a front row view." She twisted me around and tucked me under one arm so I could see the stage.

But if Hermione had one more chance to put her plan into action, I had one more chance to stop her. I squirmed around, trying to bring my now-sharp teeth or claws into play, but clearly Hermione was a cat person. She had me locked in a clinch tighter than two college wrestlers trying to conceal mutual erections. I couldn't bite her. I couldn't scratch her. In desperation, I deployed the one weapon a cat holds in reserve.

I shed. I shed all over her.

Suddenly white hairs were everywhere. They drifted like snow in the air; someone nearby gave a strangled cry and started to wheeze. In an instant, the pristine black of Hermione's tailored tuxedo was speckled salt and pepper. Hermione shrieked and held me away from her.

It was the opening I needed. In an instant, I had wriggled free and dropped to the ground. I heard Hermione curse but I didn't look back at her. The music for Mitzy's opening number (ironically a cover of David Bowie's "Changes") was starting, and I knew Hermione would choose her revenge over pursuing me. I scrambled away through the crowd, dodging feet and heading for the only ally available to me at the moment: Tarik. We may have just met, but he was about to get a crash course in what it meant to be my friend.

The space around Tarik's bar was crowded with people topping up their drinks before midnight. Being a cat had its advantages though, and I don't think I've ever made it to the front of a bar line as quickly. Choosing a man wearing the thickest possible jeans, I scaled his legs, leaped to his shoulder, and jumped onto the bar all before he could do more than yelp. My sudden appearance brought me a flurry of attention—not least from the bar manager—but I spotted Tarik and raced for him, my paws splashing through mingled puddles of beer and cheap champagne. Tarik saw me and his eyes went wide. Most otherworldly beings have some form of the sight and I'd counted on him at least recognizing me as one of Hermione's transformed victims. Fortunately, he did one better.

"Derby?" he gasped.

I slid to a stop in front of him. "You need to come with me!" I said.

Apparently my luck only went so far, though. Tarik didn't understand me at all. Instead, as the bar manager came charging after me with a broom, he grabbed the nearest salt and threw it at me. "Be undone!" he shouted. "Be undone!"

It wasn't going to work, but I could have told him that. Magic may look easy but there's more to it than just words. Also, the salt needs to be pure. The spicy mix that bars keep for rimming drinks is not an acceptable substitute.

Hacking a little bit from pepper and celery seed, I gave up attempting to talk. Instead, I turned to the stage and looked back over my shoulder with a wail. Tarik looked at me blankly. I had a sudden sympathy for Lassie and anyone who fell down a well on her watch. I didn't have any more time to try and make Tarik understand, though. Mitzy, dressed in a shimmering dress so hot and red it should have come with sirens and firefighters, was already strutting her stuff on stage. Hermione might make her move at any moment. I jumped onto the nearest customer's shoulder—fortunately she seemed to be a cat fancier—looked back at Tarik again, and wailed once more before leaping to the next shoulder.

Something must have sunk in. "Wait, Derby!" Tarik called and I glanced back long enough to see him coming after me right over top of the bar.

"Where do you think you're going?" demanded the bar manager. "Get back here!"

"Drag queen emergency!" Tarik shouted back. He snatched me up and put me on his own shoulder. "Where to?" he asked.

I craned my neck up, trying to see over the crowd. Now that I knew what I was looking for, Tarik's height made it easy to spot Hermione: she was right at the front of the crowd, with only a few people between her and the long catwalk of the stage. Mitzy hadn't gotten too close to Hermione yet—posing for the camera crew was slowing her down—but we had only moments. I sank my claws into Tarik's neck and screeched like a demon. He got the message and barrelled through the crowd toward the stage. When we were close enough, I dove from his shoulder straight for Hermione's head.

Of course, even cloaked by the glamour of the otherworldly, it is difficult for a charging satyr and a screeching cat to go completely unnoticed in the midst of a crowded drag show. Hermione turned as I leaped and managed to get her arm up between us. I hit it with all four legs and hung on like polyester blend in a tumble dryer. Seconds later, Tarik was there and trying to wrestle her down. People all around us started to complain and shove back against our struggles. A look of fury crossed Hermione's face. She gave her arm a hard snap, shaking me off, and flicked her hand. Fairy dust puffed out in a sparkling green cloud, and everyone seemed to forget all about us, returning their attention to the show. Suddenly it was as if we were fighting in our own private world, completely unnoticed by anyone.

One person could still see us, though. On stage, Mitzy blinked, and I heard her song catch ever so briefly. She'd spotted us struggling. I'm sure she'd seen Tarik and Hermione, and I hoped that she recognized me. I also hoped that she'd remember my last words to her: "Don't stop, no matter what happens." I had a plan, but Mitzy had to get closer. A lot closer.

And Mitzy, star that she is, kept on singing and making her way down the stage exactly as if nothing was wrong. I threw myself back into the fight. "Hold on to Hermione, Tarik!" I yowled. "We have to keep her back! We can't let her get close to Mitzy!"

Tarik, of course, had no idea what I was saying— but Hermione did. She fought harder than ever, dragging herself step by step toward the stage. Clearly burlesque was a better workout than I thought, because she gave as good as she got. I was only struggling to keep up appearances but Tarik was making a real effort. For a moment, I worried that Hermione might turn her magic on him. Her focus was on Mitzy now, though. We were close to the edge of the stage. Mitzy was only a few feet away, shaking the outstretched hands of adoring fans. I met Mitzy's eyes for an instant. They were frightened, but trusting. She had recognized me.

Her song hit its crescendo. I jumped away from Hermione, thumping against Tarik's chest and knocking him back. Seeing her opening, Hermione darted in. She thrust out her hand and brushed it against Mitzy's. Fairy dust shimmered—

—and Hermione vanished.

Or rather, appeared to vanish. As I crouched on Tarik's chest while he lay half-dazed among Mitzy's fans, I saw a toad as green as poison sitting just under the shelter of the stage and looking very confused. The toad's bulbous eyes focused on me. I bared needle-like teeth. The toad—Hermione, of course, her own spell turned against her—blinked, then hopped rapidly into the deeper shadows beneath the stage.

"Derby?" Tarik scooped me up in his arm. He stood and looked around. "Where is she? What happened?"

I wanted very much to answer him, or at least attempt to, but time still wasn't on our side. Mitzy, looking at me from the stage with real worry in her eyes, had finished her song and carried on with her performance. "Are you ready?" she shouted to the crowd. "It's almost midnight—count it down with me!"

"Midnight?" Tarik looked down at me. "Derby, what's going to happen? Are you going to be stuck as a cat? Should I try and find more salt?"

"Ten!" called Mitzy.

I squirmed out of Tarik's arm—"Nine!"—and wriggled up his neck.

"Eight!"

I butted my head against his chin, brushing his lips with my nose and forehead.

"Seven!"

He didn't get it. I did it again.

"Six!"

And again.

"Five!

Tarik's eyes went wide. He shifted his arms, holding me steady.

"Four!"

He kissed me.

"Three!"

Green light flashed—

"Two!"

—and I was kissing Tarik with my own lips as Mitzy and the crowd shouted out "One! Happy New Year!"

Confetti cannons went off, noisemakers trilled, and the nearly incomprehensible words of "Auld Lang Syne" filled the air, but I barely noticed. I drew out the kiss for a few seconds more before finally pulling away. "There's more than one way to break a fairy spell," I told Tarik.

"You could have said so!"

A camera light shone on us as Mitzy hopped down from the edge of the stage and pulled us both into a hug. "Happy New Year, Derby! Happy New Year, Tarik!" she said for the camera, then lowered her microphone and whispered in my ear, "What happened to Hermione?"

"She was trying to cast her spell on you the whole time," I whispered back. "But it was never going to work: you can't change the shape of a shape-shifter. When she tried, her spell bounced and affected the person closest to you instead. So your camera man, that random guy." I couldn't hold back a smile. "Hermione herself."

Mitzy gave a little squeal and slapped my chest. "You're brilliant, Derby! Help me get back on stage!"

Grinning like idiots, Tarik and I hoisted Mitzy back up. "Alright, people," she shouted into her microphone, "let's keep this party going. This is going to be a big year for Mitzy Knish and I want to start it in style!" She flung up an arm and snapped her fingers. The hard opening chords of "Surrender" by Cheap Trick blasted over the sound system. From inside the Lumber Yard, four massive bodybuilders, each dressed in the loincloth and sash of the Baby New Year, emerged onto the stage. Between them, they carried a golden throne. The crowd went wild as Mitzy took her place on the throne to finish her show.

"Damn," said Tarik. "She's something."

"She sure is." I looked over at him. "Thanks for your help. I may have cost you your job here."

He laughed. "I'm a satyr. I'm the best bartender

they've got. They'll hire me back. And look on the bright side." He winked at me, his eyes sparkling. "If I'm fired, I don't have to come in for clean-up tomorrow morning."

"No?" I asked. The tingle was back in my belly. I took Tarik's hand. "More tequila then, bartender?"

※

The party was long. The draperies around the edge of the stage parted to let in a wash of grey, pre-dawn light. Sluggish in the cold, the green toad that crouched in the shadows wriggled away from it slowly.

"Oh, come out, Hermione," said a bright young voice. "It's just me." The toad blinked but didn't move. "Come out," added the voice irritably, "or I'm sending Sara in for you."

A hiss like that of a very large snake echoed the threat. The toad blinked again, then hopped out into the light.

Four teenage girls stood outside amid the detritus of the night's revelry. Two of them, one with black hair and the other pale as age-yellowed linen, looked at the toad with bored disdain; a third, the one who held back the draperies, stared with disturbing intensity. She was a willowy redhead and her eyes were like glowing golden embers.

The fourth girl was as blonde as a cheerleader. Her nose turned up perkily, her lipstick was frosted pink, and her jacket was edged in fluffy white fur. She held a takeout coffee cup with the boxes ticked for extra foam, chocolate, and cinnamon syrup. There was a heart drawn around the name on the cup.

Bethany.

That perky nose wrinkled at the sight of the toad. "That is so not a good look for you, Hermione," Bethany said. "Stand up."

The spell broke in a flash of green light and Hermione wore her own body again. She opened and closed her fists, her knuckles turning white with the strain of each motion. "I hate that bastard!" she said. "I hate him and his singing and his fake tits—"

"Derby had fake tits?" asked Bethany, raising an eyebrow.

"Mitzy!" Hermione roared at her.

Instantly, the other three girls were clustered protectively around Bethany. The red-haired girl hissed. The black-haired girl snarled. The pale girl made no noise at all, but bared sharp teeth in black gums. Bethany gave Hermione a narrow look. "First," she said, "you need to get over this prejudice. When someone is in drag, use the appropriate pronoun. It's simple. Have you got a problem? Second—" Her eyes narrowed even more. "—*do not ever raise your voice to me.*"

Her words echoed in the empty street. Dawn's light seemed to dim a little. The draperies on the stage and the banners that hung out front of the Lumber Yard shivered as if a wind blew against them.

Hermione flinched and took a step backward. "I'm sorry," she said. "I'm just—" She paused and took several deep breaths before continuing. "I'm just frustrated. Mitzy was here just like you said that he . . . she would be, but my spell wouldn't work on her! It transformed people around her. It transformed that meddling Derby Cavendish. It even transformed me. It just wouldn't work on her!"

"Well, of course not," Bethany said. She took a sip from her cup. "She's a werewolf. Can't shift a shape-shifter's shape and all that."

Hermione's eyes went wide and angry, and her fingers curled into fists again. Green fairy dust drifted out from between her fingers. Bethany watched her over the rim of her cup. The three girls around her leaned forward as if in anticipation of a fight. After a moment, though, Hermione clenched her teeth and forced her fingers open. "You . . . knew about this?" she asked.

"I hardly knew you were going to try transforming her now, did I?"

"Then I'll try something different. Tell me where she's going to be next!"

"I could. I know people who know things. They could find that out. But I have something else in mind." Bethany shooed the other girls aside and strolled over to Hermione. "You've mastered a very particular form of magic, Hermione. You proved that last night. Even if you did get a little amphibian at the end, I like your style." She put her arm through Hermione's and pulled her into a walk. "We should work together."

Hermione stiffened. "Was last night an *audition*?"

"No! Well, yes. Do you think I just told you where to find Mitzy at a time when she was particularly vulnerable for the hell of it?" She patted Hermione's arm. "I figured Derby would be there. He usually is. By the way, you didn't hurt him, did you?"

"No," said Hermione cautiously. "I turned him into a cat, but he managed to break the spell at the last second."

Bethany snorted. "Typical Derby. He doesn't just have a horseshoe up his ass—he's got the entire horse. But that's fine. I expected as much." She stopped and turned to face Hermione. "Here's the thing. You want to hurt Mitzy Knish. I want to hurt Derby Cavendish. And the best way to hurt Derby is by hurting something he loves."

"Mitzy," said Hermione with a growl.

Bethany's laugh was a silvery sound like trees shattering in extreme cold or a barrage of bullets fired through stained glass windows. "You're thinking too small!" she said. Her voice took on a vicious edge. "I want to *destroy* Derby Cavendish. I want to *break* him. I want to hurt him so badly that he'll pull the lucky horse out of his ass, cut it open, and crawl inside the carcass to shake and shiver until the end of his days!"

For a moment, the street—maybe the entire city—seemed absolutely silent. Then Hermione said, "But I get to destroy Mitzy?"

Bethany blinked and looked at her. "You have seriously got a one-track mind."

"But I get Mitzy?"

"Yes."

"Then I'm in. When do we start?"

"Oh, Hermione," said Bethany with a smile. She took Hermione's arm again and gestured for the three girls to follow them along the street. "I've already started."

2. MARDI GRAS

The various beings that exist around the edges of the world generally don't get along with each other. Behind the glamour that hides the otherworldly from the mundane are more cliques and simmering tensions than a high school prom. There are a few notable times and places where the otherworldly do mingle, though. A hot club night here. An obscure bookstore there. A bowling alley with a particularly auspicious alignment of feng shui. One of the most infamous gathering places in our city, however, is the annual Mardi Gras party hosted by the big and burly power triad of Richard, Stephen, and Michael Holden-hyphen-Williams-hyphen-Key—a.k.a. the Three Bears.

The Bears host the event as their official joint birthday party. They've been together for so many years that I suspect they've simply forgotten each other's birthdays and are collectively too proud to admit it. In any event, the party has become *the* big do of a notoriously do-less season: Valentine's Day is mostly for couples and Groundhog Day is such a terrible excuse for a celebration not even Hallmark can sell it. Many people, mundane and otherworldly, gay and straight, wait eagerly for one of the Bears' signature purple envelopes—purple being one of the three colours of Mardi Gras, of course—to arrive each year.

For a more select and exclusively supernatural group, however, the Bears' annual invitation arrives in a gold envelope. In the scheme of Mardi Gras, gold is said to represent power. For the Three Bears it certainly does. Simply put, the Three Bears know things and, like a three-headed otherworldly godfather, they're ruthless in wielding those secrets. In addition to being a celebration, the party is their way of reminding their "clients" just where the power lies. Regrets are not an option for those receiving a gold envelope.

But the Bears' velvet fist also means good behaviour at the party is guaranteed. For one night of the year, their luxurious condo is neutral ground, and denizens of the shadows who would otherwise never speak are briefly united—mostly in murmured contempt for their hosts but you have to start somewhere. That rare neutrality is the only reason I go. My invitation—Derby Cavendish and guest—arrives each year in a green envelope matching the third colour of Mardi Gras. I'd like to think that the green envelope shows a certain respect, but I suspect it's more likely a sign that the Bears are keeping an eye on me, so when I go, I always go alone.

My green envelope for the year appeared in my

mailbox on a cold, late-January day. I took it, along with the rest of my mail, into the apartment I rent on the top two floors of a lovely, creaky old Victorian. Tarik was waiting for me, stretched out on the *chaise longue* in front of the TV with a blanket, a bowl of popcorn, and a bottle of wine. We'd been seeing each other for about three weeks, and I'd discovered that wine and sex are both better with a satyr around.

With the single-minded eagerness of new love, I dropped the mail unread on the coffee table, stripped down to my tighty-whities, and joined Tarik under the blanket. "What's on?" I asked.

"*Fast and Furious*," Tarik said.

"Mmm—just how I like it," I said. He looked at me and grinned.

Sometime later, after we'd actually started watching the movie, I reached out from under the blanket and retrieved my mail. I opened the glossy green envelope first to confirm the date of the Bears' party—and the sweaty warmth under the blanket instantly seemed cold and clammy.

Someone had drawn an emphatic line under the words "and guest."

I immediately slipped the invitation back into the envelope. I had no doubt what that line meant. The Bears had connections. They knew everything. My involvement with Tarik could not have escaped their unwanted attention, although exactly how they'd found out about him I didn't know.

I did know that they weren't going to find out anything more. "Tarik," I said, "I've got a thing I need to go to in February. Sorry, but I'm not going to be able to bring you."

He shrugged without taking his eyes off the television screen. "Okay. What is it?"

I hesitated for a moment, not wanting to involve him any more than necessary, but also not wanting to lie. "Have you ever heard of the Three Bears?"

"Only in Goldilocks."

Every so often I had to remind myself that Tarik was still relatively new to the city. At least his lack of familiarity was working in my favour. "They're important and they're having a party. Invitation only."

"Okay."

That simple acceptance gave me a warm feeling inside. I scooted in close to Tarik and wrapped my arms around him. An idea was already forming in my mind. All my life, I had reacted to otherworldly threats. I had defended against them when they attacked. With one little line, the Three Bears had changed that.

To protect Tarik—to protect any of my friends that the Three Bears might try to use against me—I was going to take the offensive against the otherworldly for the first time. I needed a plan. And

I needed help. At the very least, I needed someone to be my plus-one. If the Bears were going to insist, it would just be rude to go alone.

※

That was why, when I stepped into the elevator of the Bears' condo building on a Tuesday evening a few weeks later, my dear and trusted friend Matthew Plumper skipped on at my heels. I pressed the button for the top floor, the doors closed, and the elevator rose as smooth as grease on glass. My palm was damp. I tried to wipe it surreptitiously on my pant leg, but Matt grabbed my arm.

"Oh my God, Derby!" he squealed. "The Three Bears' Mardi Gras party! Thank you for *finally* inviting me! It's too bad Aidan couldn't come too, but I've promised to tell him everything."

Aidan is Matt's nearly perfect boyfriend. "Just remember to behave yourself," I told him.

"I make no promises," he said, then looked at me sharply. "Wait. You're nervous. You're never nervous. Derby, what's going on?"

Matt might not have the snappiest elastic in the waistband of life, but he manages to keep his underwear up. He's also my oldest friend and has stood with me against zombies, spirits, and magical attacks. Unlike Mitzy Knish (who was incidentally out of town, *Mitzy's Big Year* having blown their budget to send her to New Orleans for a Mardi Gras celebration that really mattered), Matthew is solidly mundane. He knows a thing or two about the otherworldly, though. There was no one else I'd rather have at my side in tight spot. Even so, I hadn't told him everything—or really anything. I had a plan and it involved Matt, but it also required absolutely perfect timing.

"There are some things you're better off not knowing too much about," I said simply. The elevator stopped and the doors slid open. The corridor beyond was plushly carpeted and ominously quiet. "Let's just say that the party is mixed company."

Matt winced. "Lesbians?" he asked. I shook my head. His eyes went wide. "Holy shit. The Three Bears are real bears, aren't they? I mean bears that go *grr*, not bears that go *woof*."

"They're not shape-shifters, if that's what you're trying to say." We were at the door and I could hear the sounds of the party beyond. I dropped my voice to a whisper. "They're vampires."

Matt's mood rebounded. "We have vampires in the city and you didn't tell me?"

"Keep it in your pants," I told him. "They're not what you think, they're more dangerous than you realize, and they won't be the only nasty things here tonight. Behave yourself and you'll be fine." I pressed the buzzer beside the door. "And try not to gossip."

"What?" said Matt in confusion, but it was too late to answer him. My finger had barely left the buzzer before the door opened.

The Three Bears stood before us like hairy gods, their smiles dazzling against beards thick as welcome mats, their shirts—stylishly coordinated in the colours of Mardi Gras—open to reveal luxuriant carpets of chest hair. Richard, a big muscle daddy, reached out a hand like a sirloin. Stephen, chubbier and softer around the edges, offered sugar-dusted pastries. Michael, the disarmingly adorable cub of the trio—not too hard, not too soft, but just right—held up two electric-red hurricane cocktails. I felt Matt sway before the Bears' brawny good looks and steadied him with one hand while I took Richard's with the other.

"Gentlemen," I said, "a pleasure to see you again."

Sometimes appearances can be at odds with actual behaviour. Sometimes the most macho-seeming men can have more flounce than a chorus line—as the saying goes "he opened his mouth and his purse fell out." That wasn't the case with the Three Bears.

It was more like an entire collection of handbags.

"Oh, you! The pleasure is ours!" Michael made kisses in the air as he passed us the cocktails.

"Try the beignets—everyone says they're divine!" Stephen pressed the pastries on us.

"But really, we're furious with you," said Richard, passing us the cocktails, taking our coats, and handing them off to a girl who looked like she'd been hired for the evening. He gave Matt a critical once over. "This isn't the sweet thing we were so looking forward to meeting."

"Hey!" protested Matt, but I cut him off before he could say anything more.

"I'm sorry, I didn't realize you wanted to meet Tarik or I would have brought him," I told the Bears with an apologetic smile. "But I have been meaning to bring Matthew to you for years. Richard, Stephen, Michael, this is—"

I saw recognition flicker in the Bears' eyes as I spoke, and Michael finished the introduction for me. "—Matthew Plumper! We should have known!" Michael slipped an arm around Matt's waist. "Darling, I have heard so much about you. . . ."

Matt had time only to throw me a confused glance before the Bears swept us into the party.

It was, as it always is, a who's who of the city's what-what. Matt's eyes glazed over at the sight, but I knew better. As Richard hustled us along in a flurry of introductions, I let my vision go out of focus and looked at the crowd again. A moderately famous actor chatted casually with an award-winning writer—and a pair of misty wraiths wearing festive jester hats. A pack of pixies hung out by the baby grand, their presence putting the instrument out of tune and causing the unsuspecting pianist no end of frustration. A local newscaster with a predatory reputation leaned in close to an ogress, who looked uncomfortable and scanned the room for an escape.

I didn't try to spot all of the otherworldly. Whether they had received purple envelopes or gold, most of the Bears' guests were regulars. Vampires are notoriously predictable, sticking with the same things year after year. I think it has something to do with living so long. There were some new guests, though—including a few mundanes whose true features were also concealed by glamour. That was highly unusual. I commented on it.

"Stephen found this lovely old witch in Chinatown who makes charms that are next best thing to invisibility," said Richard. "Even otherworldly don't see through them unless they try." He gave me a penetrating look. "I'm surprised that you can."

"I wouldn't be where I am if I couldn't see through charms—but it helps that I know the witch you mean. You need to careful about witches. They'll turn on you."

Richard waved my warning away. "She wouldn't

dare. Anyway, we just *had* to wring a few out of her. We've never been able to put mundanes on our special guest list before."

I didn't know most of the disguised mundanes, but there was one I recognized immediately: lurking on the fringe of the party and looking uncomfortable in his Mardi Gras beads was Reverend Bobby Gold. I must admit, I wasn't surprised to find him at the Bears' party. A fiery young preacher, Bobby had landed in the headlines not long ago after he was allegedly filmed in a motel with several other men enjoying the kind of spit roast you don't find at a church picnic. The headlines and the video had both vanished after suspiciously convenient evidence put Bobby at a prayer meeting instead. I'd suspected at the time that the Three Bears had been involved. Now I was certain of it.

Richard noticed me noticing the fallen reverend and whispered, "Don't stare, Derby. He thinks no one can recognize him."

"Does he know about—?" I tapped a finger meaningfully against my teeth.

"Naturally," said Richard. "You think that little romp in the hotel is the only thing keeping him in line? These hypocritical types have so much trouble handling the truth about themselves that the truth about the world completely blows their minds. But he'll come around. Really, we're doing him a favour.

It turns out that beneath all that bluster, Bobby is a kinky little fucker." He smiled at the preacher, who nodded stiffly in return. Without turning his head, Richard added, "He's wearing an assless rubber singlet under his clothes right now. You can give him a go later if that's what you're into."

"It's not and you know it."

Richard shrugged. "You can't blame a girl for trying. How about your little friend? No? Too bad."

"Oh, be nice!" said Stephen. A server emerged from the kitchen with an ice-lined tray of freshly shucked oysters. He waved her over. "Try these, Derby, then tell us how you've been." Stephen took the tray from the server and led by example, knocking back two of the mollusks before offering them to me. "We've heard so many things they can't possibly all be true."

I took the tray and chose my words with care as I looked over the oysters. "I suppose that depends what you've heard."

Stephen and Richard giggled in unison, then stiffened like dogs spotting a squirrel. "Doorbell!" said Stephen. "New guest!"

"Be right back!" said Richard.

"Keep the motor running," Michael told Matt, then all three Bears were flitting away.

"Vampires?" Matt asked.

"I told you they aren't what you think."

"That's for sure."

"Judgey."

"That's not what I meant," said Matt. "What was with oysters? Vampires are supposed to only drink blood."

"That's what just about everyone believes. But fresh oysters are still alive if you get them right after they're shucked and apparently that's close enough. The Bears go through them like shooters every year." I offered the tray to Matt. "Did you tell Michael anything?"

"No, but only because I don't know anything—he pumped me like cheap gas." Matt fixed me with a baleful glare. "Spill, Derby."

There was no helping it. Leaving Matt entirely in the dark now would only put him in danger, so I told him about the Three Bears' blackmail network and the special guests at the party. Matt cursed, then screwed up his face and looked around. The ogress noticed and gave him a coy smile. Matt shivered.

"Now, now," I admonished him. "Ashley may have terrible gaydar but she's lovely. The Bears are the ones we need to worry about." I offered him the tray again. "Have an oyster."

Eyes still sweeping the room, Matt took one and slurped it back without paying much attention—then made a face. "Ugh," he said. "Sand in the shell."

"Impossible. I know the caterer, Thoe. She's a nereid so she knows her seafood. She'd never let that happen." I tilted the tray to catch the light, but Matt was right. Several of the remaining oysters had visible grit around the meat. Instead of being dark, however, the grains were bright and metallic. Matt blinked.

"Is that silver dust?" His eyes went wide. "Derby, is someone trying to kill the Three Bears?"

"If they are, they're doing a lousy job of it," I said. "Silver only hurts the undead in films and bad novels. It doesn't take much to find that out—we're dealing with someone who can't be bothered to do research. That's just unprofessional."

"Wait," Matt said. "If the Bears are as nasty as you say, would it be so bad if someone did manage to kill them off?"

"It's not so simple as that," I said. "The Bears are prepared and they've made no secret about it: if they die, every bit of dirt they have on anyone floods out into the world. If they go down, everyone goes down. No one can kill them and everyone has an interest in keeping them, to use the term loosely, alive."

"Including you?" Matt asked quietly.

The question left me thunderstruck. I stared at Matt in silent surprise. He rolled his eyes. "Give me some credit, Derby. How long have I been your friend? I can tell when you're up to something. You've been avoiding bringing me as a guest to

Bears' party for years, even though I've begged you and the invitations clearly say 'and guest'—yes, I know about that. Then suddenly you invite me this year, but the first thing the Bears comment on when I'm through the door is that I'm not Tarik. You're trying to protect him, aren't you?"

"Yes," I confessed.

"And you wish you were the one trying to kill the Bears."

"I told you, Matthew, no one can kill them without putting everyone they're blackmailing at risk."

"Well, somebody clearly doesn't have your moral compass, Derby Cavendish," said Matt. He pulled me into a quick, proud hug. "Besides which, I happen to know that you would never be capable of killing anyone."

"You're absolutely right," I said with complete honestly. "Killing the Bears wasn't something I ever considered."

Bless Matt, he can be perceptive but he doesn't always look below the surface. He stepped back with a smile on his face. "So what do we do about this silver dust?"

I sighed, trying to put on a show of reluctance. "We tell the Bears about it."

※

Across the party, Richard, Stephen, and Michael were still in the process of greeting their newest arrival. Matt latched on to my arm as we approached. "Derby!" he whispered. "That's—"

"I know." I shook him off. Richard spotted us and made a show of waving us over.

"Matthew, Derby," he said, "this is another first-time guest to our little party. A mutual friend—you know Ashley, I think—suggested we invite him. His name is Horse."

"We've met," I said and shook Horse's hand with an affection I didn't need to feign. To mundane eyes, Horse looks like a massive bodybuilder. With the veil of glamour stripped away, he's an even more massive minotaur with heavy horns and only slightly bovine features. We met under difficult circumstances a couple of years ago. Specifically, he'd been transported into a cursed Christmas tree labyrinth to kill me. We'd come to an understanding however, and had instead spent the night huddled together for warmth with the added bonus of sex so mind-blowingly hot that we'd actually renewed our acquaintance a few times since. DTF, NSA, NSFW, BBC. He's not called "Horse" for nothing.

Unfortunately, duty called. Horse didn't seem put out when I said we needed a private word with the Bears. Michael picked up on the urgency and led us to a small, quiet den off of the main party. After we'd evicted a few people getting a head start on earning their Mardi Gras beads and had closed the doors, I showed the Bears the silver-laced oysters and outlined my concerns. There was a moment of silence—then the claws came out. Figuratively speaking, that is. The Three Bears are careful about revealing their true nature in public, though even they have their limits.

"Who is it?" spat Michael. "I will scratch the bitch's eyes out."

"I *thought* the first one I ate was gritty!" said Stephen. "But I saw the oysters come out of the kitchen. No one had a chance to tamper with them."

Richard snarled. I think I saw a hint of fang. "Thoe!" he spat. He turned for the door.

"Easy!" I told them before things could get completely out of control. "That doesn't make any sense. Thoe would certainly know better than to attack vampires with silver. Someone else must have done it."

"One of her staff?" said Stephen.

"Thoe wouldn't let anybody mess around with her oysters," I said. "It's more likely one of your guests. Someone who's figured out what you are. Maybe someone who thinks they don't have anything to lose."

"And it has to be a mundane," said Michael. "Derby is right. No otherworldly would try attacking us with silver. But that still leaves two-thirds of the guest list!"

As one, the Three Bears turned to me. "Derby, what should we do?"

Apparently, this is why I got the green envelope. "Think like a mundane," I suggested. "Why would a mundane try to use silver to kill you?"

The Three Bears looked at each other—then turned to Matt. He yelped and shrank back. "It's okay," I told him. "I never thought I'd say this, Matthew, but you're the most average person in the room right now. How would you kill a vampire?"

"Umm—stake through the heart?"

"Not practical at a party," I pointed out.

"Sunlight?"

Michael sneered. "At night?"

"Garlic?"

"Old wives' tale."

"Crosses?"

"Puh-leeze." Stephen wrinkled his nose like the suggestion had a bad smell. "Crosses, Stars of David, prayers—they all need true faith to work. The last time I saw true faith was a Star Wars fan with a Jedi robe and a plastic lightsaber."

"That might be something, though," I said. "Crosses are well-known weapons against vampires, but our amateur hunter went with silver dust in the oysters instead. Why?"

"He could dust the oysters anonymously," said Stephen. "If he wanted to use a cross, he'd need to confront us."

"Because he *knew* the cross wouldn't work." Richard bared his teeth and this time his fangs were fully visible. No one who'd seen him at that moment could have mistaken him for anything other than a predator, no matter how many purses dropped out of his mouth. Matt stepped behind me and I found myself wishing I had some cover as well. We weren't the target of Richard's rage, though. "Bobby Gold. He's lost his faith if he ever had any and the charm we gave him tonight would have let him slip into the kitchen unnoticed!"

Stephen and Michael had started showing their teeth as well. "Is he so desperate that he'd risk killing you?" I asked.

"I wouldn't put it past him," said Richard. He jerked his head, and the others moved toward the door.

I swallowed my fear and stepped in front of the three angry bears. "Calm down. If you go out there now, Bobby won't be the only one to know the truth."

Richard just shook his head and picked up the tray of silver-tainted oysters. "No one will see anything. You've done us a favour tonight, Derby, but this isn't your concern anymore. Lips together, girls—we're going hunting."

They brushed past me like wind in the night. I whirled and followed them back out of the den, Matt once more on my heels.

The party continued unabated. Bobby Gold stood moodily by a window. The Three Bears drifted through the crowd like wolves surrounding their prey. Matt and I stuck to Richard, so we were close enough to hear him when he slid up to Bobby and whispered, "Nice try, traitor."

Bobby flinched and the Bears closed around him. "Let me give you some advice," Richard continued. "If you're going to try and destroy someone, make sure you do it the first time."

If there's one thing popular preachers and deeply closeted gays have in common, it's a superhuman capacity for immediate denial. "I don't know what you're talking about," Bobby said stiffly.

Richard's face twisted. He took a step back and upended the tray. Ice, oysters, and silver dust splattered across Bobby—and those unfortunates standing a little too close. People around the room turned to stare. Richard, back in a frenzy of fury, ignored them. He followed the oysters with the tray itself, as well as a screaming accusation. *"You think you can cover this up?"*

"We will *break* you!" snarled Stephen.

"You tried to kill us at our own party!" howled Michael.

The collective gasp of the watching crowd could have sucked the air of a minivan. "Oh, fuck," said Matt.

"As long as they don't put out their fangs, it's just a catfight," I whispered back to him.

"Can you do anything? Bobby Gold is a shit but he can't go down like this."

I resisted the temptation to point out that going down was what brought the fallen reverend low in the first place. I looked at the three vampires, their burly chests heaving with fury, and Bobby, dripping with melted ice and oyster juice. "Just a bit longer, Matthew," I murmured, watching the scene closely. "Just a little bit longer. . . ."

Matt's mouth dropped open. "Derby, were you expecting this? Christ on a stick, you *were* expecting it! What's going on?"

"The beginning of the end for the Three Bears," I said tersely. I was literally standing on my tiptoes, poised to intercede. My entire plan depended on the next few moments.

It happened exactly as I hoped it would.

Almost.

Bobby raised his head. His face was flushed. "Really?" he said. "Well, why wouldn't I? If I lose it all,

it's better than being a bitch for you bloodsuckers!"
He reached to his neck and tore off a chunky little
talisman on a red cord—the disguise charm that
the Bears had forced out of my witch friend in
Chinatown.

The crowd's second gasp was louder than its
first as the infamous Reverend Bobby Gold stood
revealed. Some of the guests began to boo and
taunt the disgraced preacher. Many others reached
eagerly for cellphones to record proof of the juicy
moment. I saw a different look on the faces of the
Three Bears' otherworldly guests, though: hope.
Bobby had publicly defied the Bears and if he had
the strength to do it, maybe they did, too.

Stephen and Michael must have seen that look as
well. They shared one worried glance, then leaped
for Richard, trying to calm him down. Richard
was already charging at Bobby, though, his fingers
making claws and his lips drawing back. I jumped
too, ready to drag the enraged vampire down.

But a strange peace had come over Bobby Gold's
face, the peace of someone who has finally embraced
the truth about themselves. "I'm gay," he said and
looked straight at Richard as the vampire descended
on him. "And you can't use that to hurt me!"

The brilliant light that flared suddenly around
Bobby caught everyone, even me, by surprise. It
appeared out of nowhere, golden as the sun rising

after a long and dark night. It reflected in glittering sparkles from all of the tawdry purple, gold, and green decorations of Mardi Gras and made tiny rainbows in every piece of glass. The moment couldn't have been gayer if there'd been a disco soundtrack and a unicorn.

Bobby Gold had, it seemed, found faith again—in himself if in nothing else. And it couldn't have come at a worse possible time.

Richard, caught in the full blast, burst into flame instantly. Howling in pain, he stumbled back as if he'd hit a wall. My shadow fell over Michael and Stephen, partially shielding them, but they still flinched away as their flesh began to smoke. The gasp from the party crowd was the loudest yet, like a power top taking it up the ass for the first time. It turned quickly into screams as flames spread from Richard's thrashing form. The golden light winked out, leaving Bobby dazed and staggering.

This most definitely was *not* part of my plan.

It shames me to admit it, but for a moment I actually considered letting Richard burn. He was in many ways the leader of the Three Bears. Without him, Stephen and Michael wouldn't be the same threat. But I couldn't do that, not even to the Bears. I'd come to protect Tarik from them; how could I face him knowing that I'd destroyed their love to save my own?

I whipped a tablecloth from under a full buffet without upsetting a single dish and flung it to Michael and Stephen. "Put Richard out, then get him into the den!" I ordered. I grabbed Matt. "Help me with Bobby."

The fire alarm triggered and water sprayed from the sprinkler system, swiftly soaking everything and fighting back the flames. Bobby, however, just stood in the midst of the chaos, staring while the Bears' other guests ran for the door. He looked at me only when I grabbed him by the shoulders.

"What have I done?" he asked plaintively.

"What you had to do."

"What am I?"

"Whatever you want to be," I told him. "But right now you need to come with us." Matt and I pushed him toward the den. Michael and Stephen had Richard bundled up and moving as well, but in spite of the cloth and the spraying water, all three Bears were still smouldering. The light that Bobby had found within himself was not so easily extinguished.

All six of us made it into the den and I shut the door. That muffled the alarm but water still poured out of the ceiling sprinklers. Not ideal circumstances for what I was about to attempt, but there was no longer anything ideal about this situation. Stephen and Michael bared their fangs and hissed at Bobby, who pulled back. I stepped between them. "Don't touch him," I told the remaining Bears. "He's the only chance of saving Richard. Make some space."

The two vampires snarled but obeyed, shoving armchairs, tables, and a desk away like they were toys on wheels. Meanwhile, I cautiously unwrapped Richard. He was a mess, his hair singed away and his skin charred. Embers flickered and crawled in his blackened flesh, fading briefly when water fell on them only to spring back to glowing life an instant later. I looked around the room, then jumped up and grabbed a spherical crystal paperweight off the desk.

Stephen gasped. "No! That's part of a set!"

"So's Richard," I said pointedly. I took Bobby's hand and dragged him over to the burning vampire.

Not surprisingly, he resisted. "What are you doing?"

"Taking the fire out of him and putting it back where it belongs." I pulled Bobby down to his knees and placed the paperweight in his hand. "With you."

"If you save him, he'll kill me!"

"No, he won't." I leaned over Richard. "You hear me, don't you, Richard? If I do this, I want you to let Bobby live. Do you agree?"

For a long moment, there was no reaction and I almost thought that maybe I was too late after all. Then Richard's lips parted and a whisper emerged in a puff of smoke. "*Yes.*"

"Good." I put his hot, ashy hand on top of the paperweight so that he and Bobby held the crystal orb between them. Then I wrapped my hands around theirs and took a deep breath, focusing my concentration.

"Light of the sun, return!" I commanded. "Light of life, return!"

I felt something push within Richard's flesh and an answering pull in Bobby's. I squeezed my eyes shut and poured my will into that connection. "*Light of pride, return!*"

Searing heat flared in Richard's hand, scorching mine as well. Before either of us could do more than cry out, though, the heat was gone. It left my palm and fingers throbbing, but Richard's skin was suddenly cold beneath mine—perfectly normal for a vampire. I opened my eyes.

The orb glowed softly from within, lit with a warm light. Bobby stared at it in wonder. I released his hand and he cradled the crystal to his chest. I looked to Richard.

He was still as black and crispy as a sausage forgotten on the barbecue, but the flickering embers had died out. He no longer smoked—nor did Stephen or Michael, crouching now on the other side of him. I let go of Richard's hand. He reached over and touched first one of them, then the other.

I know when it's time to leave a party. I helped

Bobby to his feet, then caught Matt's eye and nodded toward the door of the den. Matt didn't need a second invitation. He caught Bobby from the other side and we headed for the door.

"Derby," croaked Richard. "Wait."

I looked back to find him gesturing for me. I hesitated, then waved Matt and Bobby on. "Get down to the street," I said. I went and kneeled beside Richard. "What is it?"

His voice was rough when he answered. "I owe you. I owe you big."

"You promised me Bobby's life," I reminded him.

Richard's lips twisted into a smile. "I promised I'd let him live."

I knew exactly what he was implying. Bobby had his life but the Bears still knew his secrets—not that they were likely to be secret for much longer. But I'd been expecting that all along, even before Bobby had brought the sun into Bears' living room. "His life is all I asked for," I said. "You don't owe me anything else." I stood up and walked to the door. "Wonderful party as always, boys, but I imagine you'll want to start cleaning up. See you next year?"

"Why do you think we wanted to meet Tarik, Derby?" said Richard.

I paused and glanced over my shoulder. "Because of me."

Richard shook his head. "No," he said. "Because of *her*."

I knew who he meant from the way he said the word and the look of dread in his eye. It took a special kind of evil to put fear into people like the Three Bears. My mouth went dry. I turned around.

"Bethany," I said.

※

Matt and Bobby were on the sidewalk, trying to act inconspicuous among lingering party guests, irate building evacuees, and emergency responders. I eavesdropped as I made my way through the crowd. The events of the party were on everyone's lips, but the glamour of the otherworldly was already at work. The Bears' confrontation with Bobby had become an embarrassing hissy fit, the subject of much speculation, while the fire had been caused by an overabundance of candles knocked into a tray of exceptionally dry martinis. By some accounts, it was the best party ever—although I suspected that any of the Bears' future parties would have a much smaller guest list. I had a feeling that their golden envelopes wouldn't carry quite the same weight after this.

"That took longer than I expected," said Matt.

"The Bears had a lot to say," I told him.

I quickly took charge. We got Bobby into a cab and whisked him away to a very reputable hotel where we put him in bed with a big glass of scotch while I made a few phone calls. First thing next morning, Bobby Gold would be on television making a more public, if less spectacular, coming out. The Three Bears would try to come after him and the best thing he could do was beat them to the punch. His old life was definitely over—he'd already experienced the media's attention when rumours of his sexuality first surfaced, but now he was going to have to face the truth.

This time, at least, he was ready to own it. In fact, it was all I could do to convince him that maybe there were some things, like the existence of vampires or being able to light up brighter than a tanning bed, that the world didn't need to know about.

"Trust me," I told him. "Stick with telling them you're gay. If you want to become the proud poster boy for rubber kink and ass play, go for it. Just don't mention the otherworldly—no one will believe you, anyway."

It was very late by the time Matt and I left him. The hotel lobby was empty and the street even more so. As we waited for cabs, Matt looked over at me. "Exactly how much of what happened tonight did you plan, Derby?"

"I don't know what you mean," I said.

"I mean that Thoe the caterer sent the oysters out just when we'd get them. Horse arrived just in time to distract the Bears so I'd spot the silver dust. That's pretty remarkable timing."

"Coincidence."

"You know Horse. You know Ashley, the ogress who got him invited. You know Thoe. You even know the witch that the Bears got their charms from."

I glanced back at him. "I know a lot of people. I knew most of the otherworldly at the party."

Matt held my gaze. "When the Bears accused Bobby of trying to kill them, he said he didn't know what they were talking about. He never did admit to anything. I think he was set up. If he didn't know silver doesn't hurt vampires, how could he know they eat oysters?"

I didn't have an answer for that. Matt sighed. "There was someone who had the chance to put the silver dust on the oysters after they came out of the kitchen," he said pointedly. "Even if he knew it wouldn't do anything."

"I'm not sure about that," I said. "I'd say that little bit of silver dust accomplished an awful lot. It broke the Bears' power. It got Bobby out from under their thumb."

"By destroying his life."

"By giving him the chance to live it."

Matt sighed. "You didn't do all this for Bobby Gold."

"No. I did it to protect my friends," I said just as the cabs pulled up. I opened the door of the first one for him. "Good night, Matthew. Give my love to Aidan."

He gave me another long look before he got in the cab. "I will. Good night, Derby. Say hello to Tarik."

I stepped back and closed the door.

Matt's cab pulled away. I got into mine, gave the driver my address, and sat back. I found my phone and dialled Tarik's number.

It took a few rings before he answered. He sounded sleepy. I'm sure I woke him up. "Hey," he said. "This is later than you thought you'd be."

"Stuff happened. Party's over. I'm heading home now."

"Do you want me to come over?"

"No. I just wanted to hear your voice. I'll call again tomorrow." I hung up and my mind went back to the Three Bears' sodden, smoky den—and what Richard had told me.

"A few months ago, Bethany asked us to use our connections to find someone. Not a particular person, just a particular type of person. Out-of-towner, otherworldly, young, good-looking, charming, not too principled. She didn't say why, but we found someone for her."

"You can imagine our surprise when you started dating him."

3. ST. PATRICK'S DAY

Who is Bethany? The short answer is that she's my nemesis. I first encountered her when I was in high school. She arrived as a transfer student from somewhere unspecified but far away—the common rumour was that her parents, strangely never around, had been diplomats in the Middle East or possibly North Africa. If you believe movies and television shows, no matter how odd or suspicious new students may appear, they're really just like us once we get to know them. The moment I laid eyes on Bethany, though, I knew she was nothing like me or anyone else. There was a darkness inside her that no one but me seemed able to see and that made me even more wary. I think she recognized me as a threat, as well. I know for certain that she did after the incident with the school mascot (don't worry, he recovered and so did the basketball team).

But even I had underestimated the true depth of her darkness. After I managed to foil her ultimate scheme—I could have told the prom committee that the "Enchantment Under the Sea" theme was both clichéd and just asking for trouble—I didn't expect to see her again. I was wrong. When we ran into each other a second time several years later, Bethany was as evil and perky as ever. She didn't appear to have aged a day. We've clashed several times since then, but no matter what happens to her, she always comes back just the same.

I've tried researching Bethany's past. As best as I can tell, she gets around like the plague. Literally. I've found a record of a young sorceress matching her description living in Constantinople in A.D. 542 during the Plague of Justinian, another of a beautiful witch near Florence in 1348 during the Black Death, and a third of a mysterious "pale lady" during the Great Plague of London in 1666. She may have been in Salem during the witch trials of 1692 before moving south to the Caribbean where a rare literate pirate wrote in his diary: "24 November 1715—Today sweet Beth-Annie who reads the Bones outside the Salty Mizzen did tell Edward Teach that he would look Right Good with a Black Beard. She is a Meddlesome Wench. Mutton for dinner. Pissed out window."

In short, wherever Bethany goes—usually in the company of the three otherworldly girls she calls Sara, Rani, and Cleo—chaos follows. I've been able to trace her progress around the world at least twice since the sixth century: a trail of war, atrocity, rebellion, upheaval, unrest, and bad fashion choices. I still don't know exactly how old she is, but sometimes when she's talked about the distant past during our confrontations, it's almost as if she was there to witness it. She's a nexus of ancient darkness; the walking incarnation of malevolence; the evil queen, the cruel stepmother, and the wicked witch all rolled into one.

She's the original mean girl. And whatever she was up to, even if it was just breaking my heart, it couldn't be good.

I couldn't tell anyone what I'd discovered from the Three Bears. I didn't want to risk that Tarik might catch any hint I knew there was a connection between him and Bethany—I knew he'd disappear faster than free Viagra at a retirement home. I definitely didn't want him reporting back to Bethany when I didn't know what she was up to yet. Setting me up with a fake boyfriend might have been cruel, but it was, quite frankly, amateur night for Bethany. She was capable of much worse, and I had no doubt that much worse was coming.

So I kept my silence, waiting and watching. If Tarik sensed that anything had changed between us, he didn't let on even when I suddenly started finding excuses to spend a little less time in his company. Bobby Gold needed help with the transition to his new lives, both openly gay and secretly otherworldly. Aaron returned to town full of tales from Mardi Gras in New Orleans—"Honestly, Derby, they were just whipping them out on the street! Cocks and tits everywhere!"—and he needed help picking out costumes for the next segment of *Mitzy's Big Year*. Various old friends that I'd neglected in the blazing heat of my romance needed to be reconnected with. The tomes and artefacts in my private sanctum on the upper floor of my apartment needed organizing. . . .

Alright, I was spending a *lot* less time around Tarik. Every moment that I was with him felt like an eternity and not in a good way. Cuddling felt awkward and sex was definitely weird in a bad way. I was certain that at any moment, Tarik would realize I was holding back. The worst part was that even after several weeks of torturing myself, I still had no idea what Bethany had planned. Tarik, my best hope for finding out more, was a brick wall—if he was hiding anything at all. I started doubting my suspicions. Maybe he didn't actually know anything. Maybe the Bears had made up the whole thing for some nefarious reason of their own. Maybe Bethany was just sulking in her evil pink lair, not even giving me a second thought.

I should have known better. The end came quickly—and it began with brunch.

※

"It's gorgeous out," said Tarik. "Why don't we do a patio with Matt and Aidan this afternoon? Before things get crazy."

I perked up at the suggestion. Sunny, warm Sunday afternoons in the middle of March are rare enough to deserve celebration on their own—a drink outdoors is both a giant "Fuck you!" to the fading tyranny of winter and a hearty "Hello, sailor!" to the season of shorts and muscle shirts—but I was also feeling a particular low point in my relationship with Tarik. The opportunity to get out of the apartment in the company of other friends was a siren call. Something in Tarik's words still gave me pause, however.

"What crazy?" I asked.

"Has the great Derby Cavendish actually forgotten a holiday?" He kissed me on the forehead. "Happy St. Patrick's Day."

Clearly I couldn't have been more distracted by Bethany if she had taken up residence in my rectum. St. Patrick's Day is hardly one of the more dangerous of the ancient dates of power, but it's certainly one of the most chaotic and even more so when it happens to fall on a Sunday. The combination of a morning parade, an afternoon of day-drinking, and an evening of hard partying is like an extra-large cock—a lot of fun at the time, but you know you're going to hurt the next day.

An afternoon on a patio would, however, hit the sweet spot between the morning's family-friendly cultural cheer and the evening's "Kiss Me, I'm Irish" free-for-all. Plus, I realized, it would allow Aaron Silverman to join us as well. After blowing the budget for Mardi Gras in New Orleans, *Mitzy's Big Year* was filming a St. Patrick's day episode at home. Mitzy Knish had a turn on a parade float in the morning and a twirl on a show stage at night, but Aaron's afternoon was free. Maybe with Matt and Aidan and Aaron in his face all at once, Tarik would finally let something slip.

"Let's do it," I said and reached for my phone.

Fortunately, all three of my friends were available, and by one-thirty we were sitting on the sun-drenched patio of the gay village's favourite Irish pub, Cockles and Mussels. A server wearing a t-shirt with the pub's famous slogan "Alive, Alive, Hos!" came over to us.

"Happy St. Paddy's," she said wearily. "Just drinks or food? You're still in time for our St. Patrick's Day brunch specials: Luck o' the Irish Hash, Eggs Colleen, Blarney Omelette, Shamrock Pancakes, and the ever-popular Green Eggs and Ham."

"What's in the hash?" asked Aidan. Matt's boyfriend is a big, athletic man, and food is never far from his mind.

"Same thing that's in everything else: green."

"Does anything come without green?" Matt asked.

"Not today, honey. Not today."

"What if we ask really nicely?" said Tarik, flashing wide eyes and a brilliant smile. My heart tugged in my chest. Whatever else he might be, he was charming. Even our server, who probably hadn't fallen for a man since Santa Claus, wasn't immune.

"I'll see what I can do," she said. Since I could see that there were a few other people on the patio eating food that wasn't artificially emerald, I doubted that the request was really that onerous. We gave in and ordered a late brunch, Aaron and Aidan gamely trying out the special menu. I drew the line at our table partaking of the day's festive drinks, however. Some things really are sacred. When our assortment of Irish stouts and good solid cocktails arrived at the table, I raised my non-green martini and proposed a toast. "To friends who are family, to brothers who are sisters—may the tops be at your back and the bottoms rise to meet you. *Sláinte!*"

"*Sláinte!*" echoed the others.

"That is sweet," added another voice. "You are all so cute, I could just puke!"

We froze, our glasses still in the air. Our table was at the edge of the patio, right up against the wrought iron fence separating patio from sidewalk. On the other side of the fence, so close I could smell the artificial apple scent of her St. Patrick's Day lollipop, was Bethany. Clustered around her were, as ever, her three harpies.

And Hermione Frisson.

"Bonjour, Derby Cavendish," said Hermione in her fake French accent. "Nothing to say? Has the cat got your tongue?"

I will admit that I was shocked. Shocked not just to see them together, but shocked to see them at all. Weeks of fretting and stewing over Bethany's plans, and here she was in front of me. I was so shocked that my first reaction wasn't to demand to know what she was up to or even to comment on the green pleather cropped jacket that made it look like she was wearing frog skin.

It was to look directly at Tarik.

For the briefest instant, I saw surprise in his eyes—then his expression closed up faster than an unlubricated asshole. So the Three Bears *had* been telling the truth. I wouldn't have thought that I could feel worse for having my suspicions confirmed, but I did. Suddenly there was a fist-sized knot in my guts as if I'd fallen asleep in the sling at Squeal on red-hankie night.

Fortunately, my real friends were there. Aaron fixed Hermione with that special kind of stink-eye only people who perform live have mastered. "Hermione, you should spread your legs a little wider. A wandering fumigator might pass by and take pity on you."

Hermione glared at him. "Shave your back!" she snapped.

"Ow—harsh. Do you want to try that one again?"

The pale girl Bethany called Cleo made the dry, rasping sound that served her as laughter. Hermione turned her glare on her. Cleo bared sharp teeth and hissed. But the exchange had given me the moment I needed to collect myself. Tarik could wait—I put his hairy, treacherous ass out of my mind and focused on the real danger. "What are you doing here, Bethany? Remembering the glory days of the Potato Famine?"

Bethany popped her shamrock sucker into her mouth and spoke around it. "Maybe I'm just out enjoying the sunshine and the Irish boys with my girls."

"Hermione is well past qualifying as a girl."

The burlesque star made a sound like a high-pressure air leak. Bethany fluttered her fingers and Hermione's outrage settled back into a seething huff. "What can I say?" said Bethany. "It's spring and I'm feeling social."

"You're social the same way syphilis is social," I said. "If you're enjoying the sunshine, it's because someone else is getting a blistering sunburn. You're never 'just out'—you're always up to something. So what is it this time, Bethany? Why are you here?"

I tried to keep my voice cool. I didn't want to let Bethany—or Tarik—see my pain. I know I didn't succeed. My words came out as bitter and angry as

GREEN

a boy band break-up. Matt looked at me in surprise. Bethany's eyebrows rose and she popped the sucker out of her mouth. Her pink lips curled into a vicious smile. "Why, Derby, you're quite worked up. Is it something I said? Or have you got a hate on about something else?" She batted her eyelashes at me.

She knew. The bitch knew. I pushed my emotions down deep. "What do you want, Bethany?"

Her smile grew wider and even more cruel. "I want to see you squirm. I want to see you twisting in the wind, strung up by your own love and good intentions."

"Full points for mean," I said, "but I think you've over-estimated yourself. Setting me up with a fake boyfriend is pretty high-school petty, even for you."

The shocked gasps from Matt, Aidan, and Aaron at this revelation were clearly audible. They all looked to Tarik, who still sat as stiff and expressionless as one of his satyr ancestors on a Greek urn.

Bethany, however, only laughed with delight. "You are so narrow-minded, Derby. This may be all about you, but you're missing the big picture." She leaned over the fence, kicking one foot up behind her. "I want you to know what's coming," she said sweetly. "Because there's nothing you can do about it."

She smiled right in my face, then stood straight and took a step back. "Show him," she said.

Hermione raised a hand full of fairy dust—and blew.

A shimmering green cloud billowed up, spreading farther and faster than anything natural should have. All of us reacted instantly. I threw myself back. Matt grabbed Aidan and pulled him under the table. Aaron jumped so fast he fell over and went sprawling against the couple munching on Blarney Omelettes and Shamrock Pancakes beside us. Even Tarik, his face finally registering a measure of alarm, flung up an arm to cover his mouth and nose, as if that would stop Hermione's magic.

But nothing happened.

I whirled around, scanning the patio. All I saw were faces staring as if we'd suddenly broken into a bad flash mob dance routine. Our server glared at us and rolled her eyes as she gathered napkins to mop up our spilled drinks. The cloud of fairy dust was gone, faded away into nothingness. Matt peeked up over the edge of the table. "What just happened?" he asked.

"I don't know." I looked over my shoulder, but Bethany and her evil little crew were gone as well—naturally.

Tarik, much to my surprise, was still there, however. I turned to face him. "Derby—" he started.

I held up my hand to stop him. "Don't. I've known for the last month. You think you're the only one who can play pretend? I don't care what Bethany offered you or why you did it. Just tell me what's going on."

The other diners were still staring. I could hear some of them giggling and gossiping. To them it was just drama: two queens having it out in public, a little show to go with their brunch. I ignored them. Tarik's face remained blank. My guts clenched again. "Coming out today wasn't even your idea, was it? She wanted you to bring me here so she'd know where to find us."

"Yes," said Tarik. His voice was odd. Tight. Maybe even conflicted. Beneath the glamour of the otherworldly, his long ears drooped.

I found that I couldn't stand the sight of him anymore. "Go away, Tarik," I said. "Whatever this was, it's over. Bethany's not getting anything else from me and you certainly aren't."

To his credit, Tarik didn't put up a fight. He turned away and, under the judging gazes of the patio patrons, walked through the gate in the fence and away up the street. As the diners' attention slowly returned to their plates, Matt stepped in beside me. "It was really all a fake?" he asked quietly. "The whole thing was something Bethany set up?"

I nodded.

"Why?"

"I don't know. I've spent the last month trying

to find out." I resisted looking after Tarik. "Maybe I shouldn't have sent him away so quickly."

"Oh, no!" said Matt. "You absolutely should have! You gave him a month longer than he deserved—even with that humongous donkey dick." Matt took my hand. "You don't need him. You're Derby fucking Cavendish. You *will* figure out what Bethany and Hermione are up to."

"Uh—guys?" Aaron said in a strangled tone. "We might have a clue already."

I turned to see him taking a step back from the table he'd crashed into. In my confrontation with Tarik, I'd only vaguely registered him trying to calm the couple whose brunch he'd destroyed. It didn't look like it had gone so well. One woman had her head down on the table. The other was rising, her face twisted with anger.

No, not anger. Her face was savage. Her lips were drawn back from her teeth and she was snarling like an animal. There was a strange, mottled flush to the skin around her eyes and mouth, almost like bruising—except that it was as green as fairy dust.

"Oh, shit," said Matt.

Then the woman's partner lifted her head. Her face, smeared with whipped cream and squished bits of Shamrock Pancakes, was even more deeply mottled. The bright afternoon sun fell across eyes that had shrunk to tiny green points. She screeched and lashed out at it with gnarled fingers.

"*Oh, shit!*" Matt screamed—then he screamed again as she turned at the sound and launched herself at him.

Aidan seemed to come out of nowhere, grabbing her in mid-air and heaving her around to slam hard against the ground. Meanwhile, the first woman had charged Aaron. He redirected her with a sidestep and a hip bump, sending her sprawling into another table. She bounded up and came at him like a pro wrestler bouncing back from a sex scandal.

Once again, we had the attention of the patio, but this time people weren't just watching—they were shrieking and yelling and jumping up from their tables. Our two lady friends weren't the only ones affected by Hermione's strangely delayed magic, either. Wherever the glittering fairy dust had spread around the patio, people writhed in their chairs or on the ground as the green stain spread across their skin. In a matter of moments, more than half of Cockles and Mussels' customers were snarling, spitting, and cringing in the sun.

But I'd dealt with Hermione's transformations before. I grabbed the salt shaker off the nearest table, spilled half the contents into my palm, and flung it over the woman wrestling with Aidan. "Be undone!" I commanded.

She turned around and snapped her teeth at my

fingers. Startled, I barely snatched them away in time. This was more than Hermione's usual magic!

"Derby, quit fooling around!" wailed Matt as he fended off our server, now transformed like her customers.

Something strange was going on and I felt a tremor of unease as I remembered Bethany's parting words, "I want you to know what's coming. Because there's nothing you can do about it." I fought back the unease. I just needed something stronger.

"Mitzy!" I called. "Break me off a piece of the fence!"

Aaron, still struggling with the woman who had attacked him, nodded. With a mighty heave, he sent his adversary flying all the way across the patio—it's a good thing Aaron has tight control over his inner wolf, because he is one freakishly strong queen when he gets riled up. He wrapped his hands around one of the vertical rods and wrenched hard on it. The rod snapped right off the fence. "Catch," he said and tossed it to me.

I snatched it out of the air like a majorette's baton and spun back to Aidan just as another of Hermione's victims jumped on him from behind. Holding the iron rod high, I dashed salt over both of Aidan's attackers and proclaimed in ringing tones, "By iron and salt and the power of Patrick whose day this is—be undone!"

The rod shivered in my hand, the salt burst into a shower of tiny sparks, and I could swear I heard church bells ring. Hermione's victims collapsed across Aidan, their bodies limp but all traces of green vanished from their faces. "Okay?" I asked Aidan.

He gave me a weak thumbs-up. I seized another salt shaker and turned to face the rest of the patio. "Alright," I said, "which of you bitches is next?"

※

It took half a dozen shakers of salt to break the spell on the rest of those affected. By the time I was done, my left hand was tingling from the shivering of the iron rod and my right was itchy from salt. The patrons of the pub who had fallen under Hermione's magic didn't remember anything. Those who hadn't were, thanks to the glamour of the otherworldly, already coming up with ways to explain away what they'd seen. The majority opinion was that a gang of drunks had descended on the patio and messed the place up. I encouraged that belief and went to so far as to suggest that the ringleader was a teenage girl in a shiny green jacket.

Aside from bruises and scrapes, my friends had escaped the fight unharmed. As we sat recovering with liberal applications of cold cocktails, however, I couldn't shake a harsh misgiving. "That was too easy," I said finally.

"Oh, it was, was it?" asked Matt. He'd probably come off the worst of us: the chair he'd been using as a shield had caught on the edge of a table and flipped up under his chin. With a wet towel pressed to his jaw, he could only drink through a straw.

"Bethany said there was nothing I could do about what was coming," I told him. "That magic was stronger than what Hermione has used before, but I could still break it. I think it was just a sample of something bigger she has planned."

"*Fucking* shit," said Matt.

"Exactly." I turned to Aidan and Aaron. Aidan just held his hands up in baffled surrender, but Aaron was looking across the patio at Hermione's victims.

"Why were some of them affected and not others?" he said. "Why weren't we affected? She practically blew her dust right on us. I know she can't transform me because I'm a werewolf, but what about the rest of you?"

I shook my head. "I don't think it was a transformation exactly. It was more like a curse, and a fairy curse would have affected you just as much as any of us. But you're right—why some and not others?" I closed my eyes and tapped my nose as I tried to reason out what might have kept some of us from succumbing to the magic.

"Green," said Aidan.

My eyes popped open. "What?"

"Green food and drinks," he said. "That's what made the difference. Our food hadn't come yet and we didn't have any green drinks, but the couple next to us were both eating food from the special brunch menu. Those guys—" He pointed across the patio. "—were drinking green beer. At that table, one of them had green eggs, but the other didn't, and only the one who did changed." He looked around at us. "Don't you pay any attention to food at all?"

"Hey, I have a wardrobe to fit into," said Aaron.

"But he's right." I scanned the patio, remembering what I'd seen when we were ordering. Not everyone had ordered from the special menu. "And it makes sense. Green food. Green magic."

"Green mottling," added Matt.

I shot to my feet. "Follow me."

Inside the pub, the manager, a marvellous dyke of my acquaintance named Moe, was on the phone. "Fucking police are taking forever to answer," she said when she saw us. "Call them back," I said. I took the phone out of her hand and hung it up. Fortunately, we're on good terms or she might have laid me out without waiting for an explanation. "Moe, what are you using to colour the food today?"

Maybe she heard the urgency in my voice because she didn't argue with this apparently random question. "Something new," she said. "All natural, totally organic food dye. No calories, no flavour, just pure concentrated colour. It's incredible." She reached behind the bar and produced a squeeze bottle.

It was still three-quarters full of a bright green liquid the exact colour of fairy dust.

I restrained myself from snatching it away from her. "Where did you get it?"

"A sales rep came in a few weeks ago. A new start-up is trying to break into the market. St. Patrick's Day was the perfect chance to prove their product so they made a super sweet deal: all the dye I needed for cost." Moe chuckled like an evil billionaire. "I don't think she knew how much green food colouring we can go through today."

"She?" I said. "Let me guess: tall and gorgeous with a French accent?"

"That's her."

Hermione. "How much do you go through?"

Moe went behind the bar and heaved up a case that was still more than half-full of green bottles. Aidan whistled in amazement. Moe laughed again. "That's just the first case. I've got two more down here."

Aidan groaned.

"Moe, you can't keep using that stuff," I said. "It's not safe."

"Are you kidding? It's as safe as water. I've got a lab report from the rep right here." She pulled a piece of paper out of the box and held it up. It was completely blank, though Moe didn't seem to see that—another of Hermione's charms at work. "Besides, I'd be crazy to give it up. I'm going to sell more green beer than ever this year. Check out what it does when you mix it with alcohol."

A pint of freshly poured beer stood on the bar, ready to go out to a customer. Moe took the bottle of dye and squeezed a healthy squirt into the glass. An intense cloud of green swirled like a storm through the beer. A moment later, it started to shimmer and sparkle as if she'd dumped in a handful of glitter.

Moe chortled with delight. "This is going to be *huge*. I don't know chemistry, but I know what people like. I'm not giving up a bonanza and I'm definitely not putting myself at a disadvantage."

"Disadvantage?" I asked.

"A rep never hits just one bar. Every bar in the village bought into this stuff. Tonight the street is going to turn green!"

My abused guts, already aching with tension after the confrontation with Tarik, dropped. Every bar in the gay village would be using the magical dye and every customer would be clamouring to drink it. And that would leave every single one of them vulnerable to Hermione's curse. In a flash of foresight, I saw Hermione and Bethany strolling through the village, fairy dust billowing in their wake while their crazed victims turned on each other. There would be too many of them. I'd never be able to break the curse on each one. There would never be enough salt. There would never be enough time.

The streets would run green—and red.

I want you to know what's coming. Because there's nothing you can do about it.

I swear I heard Bethany's silvery, tinkling laugh of triumph.

4. THE END OF
THE RAINBOW

I must have fainted a little bit, because the next thing I knew I was sitting in one of the pub's chairs with my head between my knees. Someone was draping something cold and wet across the back of my neck. I sucked in air and sat upright. Aaron, Aiden, and Matt—still clutching a dripping napkin—stood or squatted around me. "I've never seen you pass out before," said Matt. "We're in trouble, aren't we?"

"It doesn't look good," I said, massaging my temples. I was intensely aware of the sounds of merriment drifting in from the patio and the street. They reminded me too much of both the danger we faced and the screaming dirt bike of a headache racing around inside my skull. I hate visions of the future. Moe had left us alone so I told the others what I'd realized and what I'd seen.

Aaron turned pale. Aidan reached for Matt's hand and squeezed it tight. "So Bethany was right," Matt said. "There's nothing we can do."

"Fuck Bethany," I said. Bracing myself against my headache, I stood up. "Just because she says there's nothing we can do doesn't mean there isn't. You told me yourself, Matthew: I'm Derby fucking Cavendish.

I'm not going to give up." The squirt bottle of cursed green dye was still sitting on the bar. I picked it up. "There's got to be something we're missing."

"We could destroy all the dye," suggested Aidan.

"Find all the dye in all the bars in the village *and* get it out past security? Even if we could, people have been drinking and eating it all day. I'll bet Hermione made sure every brunch spot on the street got a few bottles, too."

"Then what about Hermione? We find her and stop her from throwing her dust around."

"'Stop' her?" asked Aaron. "You mean . . ."

Aidan flushed. "Maybe. If we had to."

"No," Aaron said flatly. "I've worked too hard to stay human to even think about killing someone. I'm sorry, Derby, I won't do that. Even if it puts other people at risk."

I've seldom been more proud of my friends. "You're absolutely right, Mitz. It's not an option. I don't think just taking her prisoner is, either. As long as she could get free to work her curse for Bethany, she's a danger."

That thought, however, prodded suspicion in me like a poker stirring coals. "Bethany *needs* Hermione to complete the curse," I said. "Why?"

"The curse is fairy magic," said Matt. "That's Hermione's thing."

"Then why bother with the dye at all? Why not

just curse people directly? If she did that, she could affect anyone, not just people who had consumed the dye." Further stirring brought the embers of my suspicion to a red-hot glow. "Why use Tarik, for that matter? It can't be just to distract me. If I hadn't met Tarik, I would never have even suspected Bethany was up to something."

"Maybe she wanted to mess with you more than she already has?"

"I'm sure she does. That can't be the only reason, though." I held the bottle of dye up to the window. Bright sunlight shone through its emerald depths. What was it about the green liquid that tied together Hermione, Tarik, and Bethany? There had to be something. Something more than Hermione's fairy magic. Something more than Tarik pretending to be in love with me. Something more than Bethany taking her revenge by turning the gay village into a violent, crazed horde of mindless—

"Oh, you bitch," I said as the answer burst to flaming life in my mind. "You clever, evil, immortal bitch." I spun back to the others. "We need to get back to my apartment."

"What?" asked Matt. "Why?"

"Wait, Matthew. Just wait." I said nothing more to the others as we left Cockles and Mussels and drove as fast I could to my apartment. Inside, I led them to the locked door on the upper floor. Matt's eyes opened wide.

"Your private sanctum, Derby?" he said.

"Apparently not as private as I thought." I put the key in the lock and turned it. If anyone had tried picking the lock or forcing the door, they would have felt like they'd grabbed hold of the business end of a cattle prod. All I felt was a mild tingle. I wondered if it had even startled Tarik when he went through. He would have had easy access to my keys and ample opportunity to enter while I was out or asleep.

I opened the door. The room beyond was crowded with shelves piled high with books, boxes, and mounds of bundled papers, but I knew exactly what I was looking for. I gestured for the others to join me around the desk at the centre of the room and set a box in front of them. It was about a handspan wide and twice as long, with a black cord tied around it and sealed with silvery wax. When I looked closely at the seal, I could see that it had been carefully broken, then the wax re-melted. The box didn't feel empty, though. There was something in it but I already knew it wasn't what it was supposed to be.

"Bethany didn't just set Tarik up as my fake boyfriend to hurt me," I told the others. "She wanted him to get close to me so he could steal something for her." I flipped open the box.

Inside, nestled amid folds of tissue paper, lay a big, shiny black dildo. Aaron raised an eyebrow. "Bethany knows she could just buy one of those for about twenty bucks, right?"

"Not the dildo, Mitzy. Tarik would have left that so I wouldn't notice the box was empty."

But Matt knew what was really missing. "Oh my God, Derby! It's the hoohoo stick. He took the hoohoo stick!"

"The who-what?" asked Aidan.

"The *huahua*," I said, correcting Matthew's pronunciation. "An ancient artefact that Matthew and I encountered several years ago. The huahua was a fetish—"

"Dildo," said Matt.

"—used by the Mesoamerican Ximec tribe in certain rites intended to bring—"

"Fuck," said Matt.

"—the dead back to life." I gave Matt an icy glare. "You're making it sound nasty."

"It is nasty!" He plucked the black dildo from the box and waved it in front of Aidan and Aaron. "Imagine one of these, but made out of pottery with more bumps and ridges than a mutant cucumber. What would *you* call it?"

"A good time," said Aaron. He took the dildo away from Matt and dropped it back in the box. "Why would Bethany and Hermione want an antique dildo from your attic, Derby?"

"Because the huahua is meant to bring the dead back to life, but it can do other things, too. When Matt and I first came across it, someone had accidentally used the huahua to make fruitcake that turned people who ate it into zombies."

Aaron caught on quickly. "So Bethany and Hermione used the huahua to make green dye for St. Patrick's Day!" He frowned. "Except Hermione's victims aren't zombies."

"Aren't they?" I asked. "They're vicious, mindless, and practically unstoppable. Zombies turned by the huahua aren't walking corpses, just living people under a spell. And the dye isn't just huahua magic; it's fairy magic, too. That's why Bethany needs Hermione to activate the curse. We don't need to destroy the dye. We don't need to stop Hermione. We just need to get the huahua back. Once I have it—" I slapped the lid of the burgled box closed. "—I can undo the curse completely!"

Hope was rising in my heart and a plan taking shape in my mind. "Matt and Aidan, I need you to get in touch with Horse. We're going to need some muscle to back us up. Horse has a beef with Bethany so I know he'll help. Aaron, we're going to need you, too. I hate to say it, but I think you should—"

"—cancel tonight's filming of *Mitzy's Big Year*?" Aaron finished for me. "Of course. We can fake a St. Patrick's Day party performance later, but I'd rather lose the show than see one of my crew hurt."

"Thank you, Mitzy," I said humbly. "Hermione will need to be in the village to complete the curse.

I imagine Bethany will be there as well to enjoy the chaos first hand. She'll probably have the huahua with her since it gives her some control over the zombies. The ones at Cockles and Mussels didn't seem to like sunlight, so Hermione and Bethany will wait until at least dusk before they start. Maybe even later since they'll want as many people partying as possible."

"People go out early on St. Patrick's Day," said Aaron. "Peak crowds are about eight to ten o'clock."

"Then we'll meet back here for seven and have a drink to brace ourselves before we head to the village and track down Bethany."

"Wonderful," said Matt. "Cocktails at seven, homo zombie apocalypse at eight. You're never dull, Derby."

I patted his cheek. "Don't change, Matthew. Now get going. We don't have much time."

I tried to sound confident. Inside, I was anything but. We knew what Bethany was up to now, and we knew there was a way to stop her. What I hadn't reminded my friends, however, was that to get the huahua, we'd have to go toe to toe with Bethany, her girls, Hermione, and most likely several hundred zombies. And, if Bethany was keeping him on a short leash, Tarik. For me, that last possibility was the most frightening of all.

But I must have succeeded in projecting optimism,

because all three of my friends smiled and took my hand before trooping downstairs. As soon as they were gone, I let out a slow breath, went over to the old cedar chest that stored my personal souvenirs, and took out a small box from a local jewellery shop long since out of business. Inside the box was a gaudy, glitter-enamelled shamrock pendant strung on a chain sized for a seven-year-old. I lifted it up and let it dangle in front of my face.

"You want a nightmare?" I murmured to myself. "What do I wear to fight an undying sorceress?"

※

Seven o'clock. We gathered in my apartment, our spirits high, our loins girded, and our cocktails cold. Aaron made a suitably dramatic entrance, of course, striding up the stairs from my front door in full regalia as Mitzy Knish with a vibrant red wig, stunning eyes, cheekbones for days, and an astounding kelly-green leather catsuit.

"Good Lord, Mitzy," I said as she turned for us.

"I had it in the closet from my biker days," said Mitzy. "You like it?"

"You know we'll likely be fighting?"

"I wore practical shoes." She kicked up a pair of calf-height wedge heel come-fuck-me boots. "Drag is my battle dress, Derby."

"You look fabulous."

"Good." We air-kissed. "So do you."

"Thank you." In the end, I'd followed the advice that had served me so well on that fateful St. Patrick's Day many years ago: all black with one green accessory. I wore my best narrow pants, a freshly pressed black shirt, and a sharp, tailored jacket. Strung on a new gold chain, my old shamrock pendant hung around my neck. I'd had a nagging feeling that I looked like some kind of Irish Satanist, but Mitzy's blessing erased that fear and gave me a new confidence. Maybe we would be able to pull this off after all.

"So are we ready to go?" asked Matt.

"Not quite. I called in one more person to help. We're waiting for—" My doorbell chimed before I could finish. I trotted downstairs to let in the last member of our valiant band.

The others blinked in unison when I returned with Bobby Gold.

"Hi," he said nervously.

"Really, Derby?" said Matt.

"Absolutely," I said. "Bobby, introductions—" I went around the room with names, then again with the information that might not have been immediately obvious. "Mundane, mundane, werewolf, minotaur." I ended back on Bobby. "Secret weapon."

Mitzy's eyebrows rose. "In good time, Mitz," I said, then lifted my glass in a final toast. "Luck of the Irish!"

The others echoed me. I tossed back the last of my cocktail and set the glass down. "Now," I said, "let's kick Bethany's pert little tushy."

The village was crowded when we got there. Lesbians and gays of every stripe—along with party-loving representatives of every other letter in the alphabet soup of queerness—crowded the sidewalks. Every conceivable watering hole was filled to capacity, which meant long lines of people waiting to get in. The street hadn't been formally closed to traffic, but so many people were walking on the road that police and drivers seemed to have just given up in frustration.

"This is busier than I've ever seen it on St. Patrick's Day," said Mitzy.

"I think Bethany and Hermione encouraged it." Aidan picked a battered postcard off the ground. ST. PATRICK'S DAY IN THE VILLAGE, it read. SHOW YOUR PRIDE. SHOW YOUR LOVE. THE PARTY TO END ALL PARTIES. FREE SHOW BY BURLESQUE SUPERSTAR HERMIONE FRISSON.

"It gets worse," Matt said and pointed.

On a street corner nearby, a young woman in a t-shirt sporting the logo of a well-known chewing gum company was handing out samples. "Free super mints," she said in a droning, mindless chant. "Free super mints. Super green, super fresh. Free super mints . . ."

The samples she was passing out were in clear packets that carried no logo at all. Even from a distance, I recognized the shimmering green of the cursed dye in the mints and the blank expression of someone under a fairy enchantment. Bethany and Hermione had even found a way to get the dye into people who weren't drinking! "Damn it!" I cursed and strode over to the young woman. She tried to hand me a mint.

"Free super mint—"

"No!" I had filled one pocket of my jacket with salt in case I needed to break one of Hermione's spells. I flicked some at the young woman. "Be undone!"

She staggered and blinked, looking around in confusion. I walked on—she'd come up with her own rational-seeming explanation for whatever missing time she'd spent under Hermione's charm. Judging from the number of wrappers littering the street, it had been a while. And she likely hadn't been the only one.

"We need to split up to look for Hermione and Bethany," I said. "Matt, Aidan, and Horse: take the far side of the street. We'll take this side. Check everywhere. Ask door security if they've seen them. Don't get too far apart. If you see anything, call for help."

Our group divided. Mitzy, Bobby, and I slowly made our way up our side of the street. The spread of the huahua-tainted dye was frightening. Through the windows of every bar, I could see people drinking mugs of green beer. In the queues outside every door, people were popping the free mints. My favourite hole-in-the-wall sushi place was serving up green rice and somehow the dancers at the village strip club, Hang-Out, had discovered the dye made a fine body paint. They loitered shirtless outside the club, green designs drawn on their naked abs and pecs, and invited customers in for free lessons in art appreciation. Bobby, still discovering the wonders of gay life, was drawn to them like a moth to cashmere. I drew him back again. "Focus, Bobby!"

There were no signs of Bethany or Hermione. I asked the door security at every bar if they'd seen them. Mitzy asked everyone we saw that she knew— which was a lot of people. No one had seen them, but everyone was looking forward to Hermione's show.

"Do you even know who she is?" Mitzy demanded of someone just outside the Lumber Yard.

"No, but I want to see her!"

Mitzy snorted. "Fairy magic," she whispered to me. "It has to be."

"Hey, Derby!" One of the bartenders from the Lumber Yard, outside having a smoke break, waved me over. "Where's Tarik? He was scheduled to work tonight but he didn't show up. The boss is pissed."

I met the question with as much grace as I could muster. "I don't know where he is. We broke up today. He did something unforgivable."

"What? No! Not Tarik—not to you. He was head over heels."

He actually seemed to believe it. "He lied," I said. "He betrayed me."

"He cheated? No way. Do you know how many guys threw themselves at him every shift he worked? Tarik turned them all down."

"He didn't cheat on me." The conversation was starting to annoy me. I knew I should just walk away and keep looking for Bethany and Hermione, but the idea that someone—anyone—could defend Tarik made me angry. "He stole something from me."

The bartender looked surprised and a little crestfallen. "Oh. Well, I guess that would explain . . ." He hesitated, then added, "A bit more than a month ago, Tarik came in looking really down. He didn't want to talk about it or you. I figured you'd maybe had a fight. It took a week before he was himself again. Whatever happened, he felt like shit about it." He took a final drag on his cigarette, then crushed the butt under his foot. "I've got to go back in, but listen, you have to talk to him about this. You have to give him another chance. He loves you."

And he walked away as if he hadn't just delivered the second biggest gut punch of my day.

"Derby . . ." said Mitzy.

I held up my hand to stop her, then took a deep a breath and let it out slowly. "I'm okay," I said after a moment. "Let's find Bethany."

But Matt found her first.

We were just past Squeal when my phone rang. The caller ID showed Matt's name but I didn't even have a chance to say hello before he was screaming, "She's behind us! *She's behind us!*"

I spun around, phone still to my ear. Down at the south end of the village, close to where we'd started our search, a hazy light had sprung up in the middle of the road. No, I realized, not hazy. It was actually bright and sharp, like a portable spotlight. The haze came from the green dust spreading in a cloud around it.

"We'll meet you there!" I said, and we were off back the way we had come. The light and cloud were part of a small procession that led a dancing, cheering mob. Matt and the others found us and we made our way through the growing crowd.

It was them, of course. Hermione strutted at the head of the procession in a sexy little mini-kimono and silk stockings that had nothing to do with St. Patrick's Day other than being green. She was tossing out handfuls of fairy dust pulled from an open sack carried by a half-naked young man in green tights who watched her every move with slavish devotion. A second enchanted slave lugged the spotlight that flashed back and forth in the sparkling green cloud. A third slave held a powerful little portable stereo that boomed out "Applause" by Lady Gaga.

"Tacky," said Mitzy, but I barely heard her. Immediately behind Hermione and her slaves walked Bethany, her girls, and—I sucked in my breath in spite of myself—Tarik.

I felt Matt grab my hand.

Bethany walked as if she didn't have a care in the world. Sara, Rani, and Cleo, on the other hand, prowled like animals, their eyes darting back and forth through the crowd that danced around them. Tarik was scanning the crowd, too, except he didn't look predatory. He looked, I realized, scared.

"What do we do, Derby?" Matt shouted in my ear.

I clenched my jaw. "We take the offensive," I said and pushed right up to the front of the crowd. "Bethany!" I bellowed above the music. "Give up the huahua!"

For a moment, the procession froze. Bethany stiffened in surprise—clearly she hadn't been expecting I'd figure it out—and shot an accusatory glance at Tarik. But Tarik was staring at me with a wild, desperate look in his eyes.

"I'm sorry, Derby!" he blurted—then leaped at

the slave boy carrying the sack of fairy dust, tore it from him, and raised it high, ready to hurl it away.

Quick as thought, Hermione spun around and blew a puff of dust straight in his face.

Tarik blinked once before his expression went completely blank.

"Hermione, go! Get to the intersection. Girls, stop them!" Bethany shouted, but Sara, Rani, and Cleo were already charging us. Rani, screaming like some kind of great cat, clipped the young man with the stereo as she passed. He went down. The stereo crashed to the pavement and the music stopped.

The crowd didn't stop dancing, though. Or rather they didn't stop twisting and writhing as the green stain spread across their skin. The curse of the huahua was taking hold!

I caught a glimpse of Hermione dragging Tarik off into the crowd, trying to get around us and farther up the street, then Rani, Cleo, and Sara were on us. I always knew that Bethany's girls were something more than human but this was the first time I'd really seen them in action. Horse confronted Rani and took a swing at her. If he'd connected, the blow probably would have lifted her clear off the ground, but Rani ducked under the punch with an easy grace. She swiped at Horse with fingers that suddenly bore sharp claws. He pulled back to avoid her, but not quite fast enough. Four big slashes opened up across the front of his shirt. Meanwhile, Mitzy gave Cleo a high, sweeping kick. Cleo blocked it with a raised arm. Mitzy might as well have been kicking an old heavy training bag; all the impact did was raise a puff of grey dust from Cleo's arm. Cleo grinned, showing teeth and black gums, and grabbed for the raised leg, but Mitzy hopped back and Cleo's fingers closed on air.

Sara came gliding at us between the battling duos. She swayed as she moved, her eyes so intense they were almost glowing. Matt and Aidan stepped up to meet her, one on either side, dividing her attention. Bobby hesitated, as if he might join them, but I grabbed his arm. "Stay with me," I said. "I need you close."

"I see you back there, Derby!" called Bethany. "I really hoped you would try to stop me. It makes things so much more interesting—and I'll enjoy it so much more when you fail!"

"I'm not finished yet, Bethany!" I shouted back. Around us, the St. Patrick's Day crowd was starting to move as people realized something was wrong. The first ripples of panic were slow. Those few who hadn't consumed the cursed dye tried to help their stricken friends.

Then the zombies attacked.

Terror tore through the crowd. The zombies were like a wave pushing up from the south end of the village where Hermione's little procession had started and driving the fortunate unaffected before them. They poured out of Hang-Out and the Lumber Yard. I recognized many of them: Moe from Cockles and Mussels, the bartender who had asked about Tarik, my barber at Manly Man Salon and Nails. Bethany's silvery laugh rose over the screaming. She appeared above us, casually walking up onto the roof of a car parked at the side of the road.

"You *are* finished!" she yelled mockingly. "You might have stopped a few zombies this afternoon, but you know you can't fight this. And the best part is you made it possible because you fell in looovve!" She laughed again, then leaped high into the air, passing over our heads to land lightly on the roof of the next car.

"She can do that?" yelped Bobby.

"I don't regret it!" I told Bethany. "Love makes us stronger!"

"You sound like a pop song! You don't even know what you're facing yet." She clapped her hands. "Girls! Play time is over!"

She spun around and jumped car to car up the street in the same direction Hermione had run. Sara, Rani, and Cleo broke past us an instant later, carving through the growing chaos as they followed her.

I pulled Bobby off the street and into the cover of

the deep-set doorway at Manly Man. Matt and Aidan joined us, with Mitzy and Horse, slightly battered but largely unharmed, close behind. "Derby, what did she mean we don't know what we're facing?" Matt asked.

I popped my head out from the doorway, staring at the zombies rampaging along the street. They seemed more vicious than the ones we'd faced at brunch, chasing the people who fled from them, dragging them down—and chewing on them. A horrible fear grew inside me, one that was confirmed as a sobbing young lesbian stumbled into our refuge.

"What's happening?" she gasped. "This isn't possible. This isn't possible!" She was holding one arm close against her body. Her sleeve was torn and bloody. I could see the flesh beneath.

The bite marks were already turning green around the edges. The curse of the huahua wasn't just being spread by green beer and fairy dust anymore.

A zombie screeched close by. The young woman screamed and scrambled back out into the street, but that only attracted the attention of her pursuer. Another woman wearing a t-shirt that read "Bend over backward and kiss the Blarney!" leaped into view and slammed her to the ground—then paused and stared at us with sunken, green eyes.

"Bobby," I said without looking away from her. "Do it now."

Out of the corner of my eye, I saw him pull the crystal paperweight from the Three Bears' den out of his pocket. His movement drew the zombie's gaze. She bared bloody teeth and took a step toward us.

I held up my hand, fingers stretched wide, in a gesture of forbidding. The woman with bloody teeth hissed, then screeched. Other zombies shrieked in response. The woman crept forward.

I could see Bobby cradling the crystal sphere in his palm. I could hear him whispering to himself, "I'm gay and I'm proud. I'm gay and I can do this. I'm gay and—"

Horse leaned in, pulled Bobby's face around, and stuck his tongue so deep into his mouth that Bobby's whole body went stiff.

The crystal burst into the same dazzling, golden radiance that had burned the Three Bears. The zombie wailed and reeled away from the light. Other zombies, caught in the spreading glow, howled and pulled back as well—exactly as I'd hoped they would. My secret weapon had worked.

"Everybody out!" I commanded. "We need to go after Bethany and Hermione. Bobby—good work."

Bobby, still looking slightly dazed from Horse's inspiring kiss, nodded numbly and started to move, then hesitated. "Uh, I need a minute," he said, one hand cupped over his crotch like an embarrassed teenager.

"We don't have one," said Matt, dragging him forward. "Own your boner, Bobby!"

Surrounded by the brilliance of Bobby's sunlight, we stepped out of hiding.

※

The scene was a little quieter now. Most of the zombies had continued on up the street after Bethany and Hermione, following the power of the huahua. Those that still lingered nearby hissed and cringed away from the light. All around us, the still-human survivors of the attack lay moaning amid the devastation of the gay village. The few who could still walk were trying to help the others to safety—except there would be no safety. My heart nearly broke, but I knew now that was exactly what Bethany had intended all along. I pressed my lips together.

"If we have to fight the zombies, try not to hurt them unless you absolutely have to," I said. "They're still our brothers and sisters. We're going to save them."

The others all nodded grimly.

Ahead of us, the street was clogged with zombies. Fortunately, the attention of the churning mass was focused entirely on the intersection that was the heart of the gay village. Something was on fire up there, belching out dark, greasy smoke that shimmered with green. I sucked air between my teeth. A crossroads was a place of power; whatever was happening had to be the cherry on top of Bethany's shit sundae. I leaped onto a parked truck to get a better look. The flames and smoke came from two cars that had collided in the intersection. The green shimmer came from the handfuls of fairy dust that Tarik—still expressionless—tossed mechanically from the sack into the fire while Hermione danced around it, her movements tracing a magic fairy circle.

Bethany stood inside the circle, right beside the burning wrecks, wreathed in smoke and fire like a cheerleader from Hell—except instead of a pompom, she held the huahua. We didn't have much time.

Smoke and fairy dust weren't the only things in the air, though. A strange kind of energy seemed to pool in the shadows and crackle around the streetlights. "What is that?" asked Aidan.

"That's the glamour of the otherworldly trying to assert itself," I said as I hopped down from the car and urged the others onward. "Bethany has stretched it too far. It's shredding like overworked tights."

"What does that mean?"

"It means that people are going to see things they weren't meant to see." I pointed at Horse. "Like that." Aidan looked—and jumped as he saw Horse's true minotaur form for the first time.

Horse wasn't the only one affected by the fading of the glamour. Mitzy was twitching and grimacing as she walked, and I knew the wolf inside her was trying to come out. "Let it go, Mitz. You'll have more control if you don't fight it all the way."

Mitzy nodded and took a breath, then tensed, stretched, and groaned. Fur swept across her skin. Her bones and joints popped and reshaped themselves. Her body stretched out, and those fabulous wedge heel boots split apart at the seams. She shook them off and scraped heavy claws against the pavement. Miraculously, the green leather catsuit hung together and the red wig ended up looking surprisingly good on the head of a seven-foot-tall wolf-man—or rather, wolf-woman. Mitzy raised her head and howled.

Bethany, Hermione, and all of the zombies turned.

With Bobby shedding more light than a high-powered dance floor, they would have seen us sooner or later anyway, so I was ready. I thrust out an arm. "Get us through the zombies, Bobby!" We broke into a run.

Bethany pointed right back at us. "Get them!" she screamed and the zombies hurled themselves at us.

It must have looked like a tugboat heading into

a massive tidal wave: our little bubble of light against hundreds of raging, tight-packed zombies. Bobby came through for us, though. He raised the shining crystal sphere high and shouted his pride and defiance. The light flared even brighter and the zombie horde parted for us like a hungry ass taking a well-greased fist.

Sara, Rani, and Cleo were waiting for us when we broke through the zombies, though, and a terrifying sight it was. The tattered glamour showed more of their true nature than I had ever seen before. Rani's black hair and green eyes had become the fur and eyes of an enormous panther. Sara's amber eyes had become those of a huge snake and her red hair the creature's coppery scales. Cleo, however, had shrivelled rather than grown, her flesh dried hard on her bones, her aged-linen skin in tatters like ancient bandages. Whenever I'd caught the hint of something long dead about her, it hadn't been my imagination. Cleo was a mummy.

But now we'd fought them before. Mitzy and Horse exchanged a glance, then each went after the other's previous opponent. Horse pummelled Cleo's leathery form, while Rani and Mitzy tore into each other with raking claws and terrible teeth. I ached to see Mitzy bleed but we had our own problems. Sara's thick body coiled and swayed as she circled Matt, Aidan, Bobby, and I. A long, forked tongue flickered past fangs as big as daggers and dripping with venom. I could feel her hiss like a tremor in my body.

It was difficult to tell where her snake eyes were focused but I had a good guess. She didn't need to take out all of us, just Bobby. With his light extinguished, there'd be nothing to hold back the zombies that snarled and screeched around us.

"What do you think of my girls now, Derby?" called Bethany. Strangely, I couldn't see anything different about her, even with the thinning of the glamour's veil. Hermione had the suggestion of her mysterious fey mentors about her. Tarik's ass ears and drooping tail were on full display. Bethany, though, was simply Bethany.

I held my head high and called back to her. "I've always wondered what they were. Where did you find them?"

Bethany laughed. "I picked them up over the years. Each of them was a queen once. Now they belong to me." She smiled. "Maybe I'll mix things up a bit and make Mitzy one of mine, too. Once you're gone."

Anger burned in me. "I'm not going anywhere." I looked Bethany straight in the eye. "You made a mistake choosing today, Bethany. It left you vulnerable. After all—" I grabbed the plastic lid of a litter bin that some zombie had torn free and flung into the street. "—St. Patrick drove the snakes out of Ireland."

I banged my hand against the lid. It was hardly St. Patrick's drum but the sound boomed out much louder than it had any right to. Sara hissed like wind in a graveyard and thrashed as if she was in pain. I hit the lid again. "Matt! Aidan! Bang anything you can find! Wait, I mean—"

"I know what you mean!" shouted Matt. He started drumming on a car hood and Aidan on a mailbox. With every reverberating bang and thud, Sara hissed and flailed. Bobby stayed close, holding the crystal sphere high so that its light shone everywhere.

"Rani! Cleo!" Bethany called, but her other two minions were in no position to help. Horse had Cleo pinned, while Rani and Mitzy rolled on the ground, each trying to rip the other apart. Hermione glanced at us.

"Bethany, I can—" she said, but Bethany cut her off.

"Dance!" she ordered. "Finish the spell! Hurry!" She kept her eyes on me. For the first time ever, I saw Bethany sweat and I'm sure it wasn't from the fire. She'd made no move to help her girls, I realized, and that seemed completely unlike her.

An idea occurred to me. I threw my lid to Aidan, dodged past Sara's heavy coils, and charged—straight at Hermione.

She squealed and flinched. "Dance! Dance!" said Bethany frantically. Hermione jumped, dancing faster, but the problem with a magic circle is that I knew exactly where she was going next. I pulled a handful of salt from my pocket, dodged to the side to intercept Hermione, and flung the salt.

"*Be undone!*" I shouted.

Hermione ducked. I don't think a single grain of salt landed on her. She came back to her feet with a sneer on her face and fairy dust in her hand, ready to flick at me. "You missed," she said.

"He wasn't aiming at you!" Bethany shrieked.

Behind Hermione, Tarik blinked and expression came back into his face. He looked at me. I nodded. His mouth curved in a wild grin and he dropped the sack to grab Hermione from behind, dragging her away from the circle. She screamed in surprise and the dust fell from her grasp. As Tarik wrestled with Hermione, I turned on Bethany.

She still hadn't moved, but if a glare could open a hole to Hell, I would have been swimming in brimstone.

"You know," I said, "I thought you were trying to get Hermione to finish a spell that would complete or strengthen the huahua curse. But the curse was already complete, so what was the magic circle for?"

I looked down at the glittering lines of the circle. Up close, I could follow the patterns. They confirmed what I suspected. "Binding magic," I said to Bethany. "Intended to hold something at bay. But it works from both sides, doesn't it? It can keep something in—or keep something out."

"Shut your hole," said Bethany, but there was fear in her eyes now. I saw her glance down at the smudged spot where Hermione had stopped dancing. The pattern of the circle was visibly dissipating, the magic unravelling.

And it was unravelling faster and faster. "You knew that a horde of zombies would be too much for the glamour to take, so you're trying to keep it intact inside that circle," I said. "That's why you look exactly the same as you always do. You don't want anyone to see the real you." I narrowed my eyes. "Or maybe it's more than that. Some things are just too otherworldly to exist. I've heard that when the glamour breaks around them, it tries to fix itself by writing them out of existence."

"Shut up!"

"Give me the huahua and I'll let Hermione finish the circle!" I said. The lines of fairy dust were fading fast now. Bethany was fading, too, and a shadowy new form taking place around her. I held out my hand. "Give it to me, Bethany. With the curse undone, the glamour will bounce back."

She stared at me. For a moment, I thought we might actually have a deal. Then she put back her head and laughed her silvery laugh. "And be in your debt?" she screamed. "Fuck you, Derby Cavendish! Fuck you and everyone you love." She lifted the huahua high. "If I'm going, I'm taking this with me!"

Without waiting for the circle to unravel any further, she stepped out of it.

I felt the strained glamour shiver around me.

Bethany's mortal form fell away. She grew tall— taller than me, taller than Mitzy—and aged rapidly from teenager to mature woman. Her face turned harsh, savage. Her hair twisted into a serpentine crown and her cute clothes faded, becoming a full, stiff skirt of patchwork leather and a tight corset that left her arms and full breasts bare. Massive dark wings the colour of storm clouds grew behind her. When she spread them, lightning crackled between the feathers.

"Behold!" she said in a voice like thunder. "Behold your nemesis!" And she laughed that same tinkling laugh but now instead of silver, it was bronze.

The glamour of the otherworldly snapped.

I felt it right through my body. Hermione's laugh turned into a wail as the sundered glamour struggled to repair itself. She started to drift apart, her fabulous wings fading into wisps of mist, her leather skirt crumbling into dust. "No! So many centuries, so many eons!" she cried, but her thundering voice was already just a whisper. She gave me a glare of pure hatred that I will never forget—and clutched the huahua tight to her breast.

"Fuck," I said under my breath. I dropped to my knees and pulled the rest of the salt from my pocket. Working fast, I poured it out of my palm into the lines of another magic circle no wider than a double handspan and much simpler than Hermione's. With my other hand, I snapped the old shamrock pendant from my neck and dropped it in the middle of the salt pattern, then closed the circle. I flung one hand into the air and pointed the other at the pendant.

"Be bound!" I called out. "Ancient of ancients, be sealed within. Nameless and unknown, your essence hidden, your secrets protected. You and you alone, be bound! Be bound!"

The wail of the thing that Bethany had become rose into a heartrending scream and her drifting substance streamed down to my open hand, along my arm, then out into the magic circle. It swirled twice around inside the boundary of the salt, then drained down into the glittering enamel of the shamrock. Bethany's scream cut off as if someone had closed a door.

The huahua smacked into my open palm. I looked up at it—and found Tarik staring at me as well. I held up my other hand to stop him from speaking, then stood and turned around. All my friends were staring at me. So were Hermione and Bethany's girls. So were all of the zombies.

I could still feel the broken glamour surging around me. I faced south, raised the huahua, and swung it through a wide clockwise circle. East to west. The passage of the sun from dawn to dusk, and back again through the night. The procession of life and death and rebirth. "Be undone!" I proclaimed.

The zombies moaned. The glamour calmed. I repeated the motion and said louder, "Be undone!" The zombies moaned louder. The glamour stretched.

I drew a third circle. "Be undone," I roared as the zombies cried out, "and never be again!" I seized the huahua with both hands and broke it in two. For an instant, the world seemed to explode in light— green light—as the curse of the huahua shattered and the glamour of the otherworldly sprang back into place.

Then it was over—and I was holding two pieces of what had assuredly been the world's ugliest pottery dildo.

5. FRIENDS LIKE THESE

Our little gay village made national headlines the next day. MOB INVASION, read one paper. UNKNOWN ATTACKERS TRASH GAY DISTRICT, read another. DOZENS INJURED, read a third, POLICE HAVE NO SUSPECTS. I saw Moe from Cockles and Mussels interviewed on a morning news program. "I don't know what happened," she said. "One minute, business was booming and everybody was happy. The next minute, it was complete chaos. Everybody was screaming and running, and there was a gang of thugs in these weird masks throwing green smoke bombs and just tearing up the street. It was like the end of the world."

How close she was to the truth! Thanks to the freshly restored glamour of the otherworldly, though, the real events of the night were quickly rationalized. By the time police, paramedics, firefighters, and anyone else driving a vehicle with sirens arrived in the village, no one remembered clouds of fairy dust, rampaging zombies, or a werewolf in drag fighting a giant panther in the middle of the street. They remembered a crowd of masked attackers appearing suddenly to terrorize their peaceful St. Patrick's Day parties. They remembered smoke bombs. They remembered dogs (responsible for the bites suffered by numerous victims), and, weirdly, cats. A few people were certain one of the attackers had carried a really huge snake as well, and maybe there'd been a big guy wearing some kind of helmet with horns on it.

Most people also recalled coming together in a big gay mob of their own to drive out the attackers, a convenient explanation that led to an exuberant, renewed sense of pride and community—which was a good thing, because the aftereffects of Bethany's plot were very real and not so easily dismissed. Nearly every business in the village was damaged and many people had been injured, some quite badly.

I'm proud to say that Miss Mitzy Knish immediately took the lead in helping those affected. Using her not-insubstantial network of contacts— and leaning heavily on those contacts to work their contacts in turn—she brought together musicians and drag artists for a fabulous benefit show that not only put the gay village back on its feet, but funded a new program for at-risk youth at the local community centre. Not inconsequentially, it also got *Mitzy's Big Year* bumped up to a more prominent network, but if you ask Mitzy she will absolutely deny any connection. Cynics might say she did it for the fame, but I know Mitzy and she did it without any thought of reward.

The police promised a swift investigation of the events of that terrible night, of course, but I knew they'd never find those truly responsible and not just because they were chasing shadows of glamour. Bethany was bound inside my shamrock pendant, beyond the reach of any mundane cop. I'd seen enough to guess at her true identity, but naming a thing gives it power, so she would always remain Bethany to me. Sara, Rani, and Cleo seemingly vanished with the restoration of the glamour. They were simply gone when we looked for them, although weeks later I heard rumours of a trio of strange, feral teen girls roaming the city's ravines.

Hermione Frisson was still with us, though—in a manner of speaking. The sudden unweaving of her magic circle, the tearing and restoration of the glamour, and the breaking of the mingled fairy and huahua magic of the zombie curse did something to her. Her eyes have turned as green as fairy dust, and most of the time they're focused into the distance on something that no one else, not even me, can see. She still dances, but she does it in a long-term care facility. Aaron and I drop by to check on her every so often. Hermione seems to have forgotten all about her rivalry with Mitzy. They compare dance routines and talk costumes, although personally I don't think Hermione's plans for a burlesque show performed entirely in sweatpants will ever go anywhere.

And then there was Tarik.

We were separated in the immediate aftermath of the breaking of the huahua as the rest of us tried to disperse the crowd of confused former zombies, but he found me again before long. "Derby, I need to talk to you," he said, then paused as if expecting me to cut him off the way I had earlier. I didn't say anything, though. I think that flustered him. He looked down at his feet, ass ears drooping.

"I'm sorry," he said. "I'm really, really sorry. When Bethany came to me and said she wanted something stolen, I didn't think anything of it. It was just a job. Then I met you." He looked up. "It was only fake at first. I fell hard for you, Derby."

"I fell hard for *you*," I told him back. My heart felt like it might tear itself out of my chest. I still stayed a step away from Tarik, however. "But you took the huahua anyway."

"I didn't realize how I really felt until after I took it. I thought I'd be okay, but as soon as I handed it over to Bethany, I completely fell apart. I felt like such a piece of shit."

"You could have told me about it."

"I was scared to." Tarik sniffled. His face twisted and tears welled up in his eyes. He was on the verge of a full-on ugly cry. "I was scared of what you'd think and I was scared of what Bethany would do to me. I knew what she could do by then. I knew what she and Hermione were planning with the huahua."

I reached out and took his hands. "You still could have told me."

A sob escaped him. "I know. I should have." He pulled one hand away to wipe his face. "I should have been gone a couple of weeks ago. That was the plan. But I convinced Bethany I should stay to keep an eye on you until the last minute. That's what gave her the idea to taunt you this afternoon. Then when you told me to go away—" He swallowed another sob. "I couldn't. I went back to Bethany and told her I wanted to help, but I was really waiting for you to come because I knew you would. I tried to help. . . ."

"You were there in the end," I said and made an attempt at a smile. "I couldn't have taken down Hermione without you."

Tarik managed to both cry and laugh at the same time. He took my other hand again. "I love you, Derby."

"And I love you," I said—then let go of him. "But you hurt me, Tarik. You betrayed me. You hurt my friends." I swept an arm around the ruined village. "You hurt a lot of people."

"Derby—"

I took his head between my hands and kissed him lightly. Once. "I love you, Tarik, but I won't stay with you."

I walked away.

Matt and Mitzy—human once more, of course, and barefoot without her ruined boots—found me sitting on the steps at Squeal. "We saw that, Derby," said Matt. "Are you okay?"

I sighed. Holding back my own tears was hard, but still easier than I'd expected. "I will be," I said.

Mitzy hugged me. "You're the best."

"Thank you, Mitzy. Your left boob is broken."

She reached inside her shredded dress, pulled out the fake tit, and tossed it away, then went back to hugging me. Matt embraced me from the other side.

"*We* love you, Derby Cavendish," he said.

My heart swelled and I did my best to hug them both back. With friends like that, I can withstand any fake-ass lover, zombie apocalypse, or undying nemesis. I'm Derby Cavendish—and I know I'm unstoppable.

PUBLICATION HISTORY

"Fruitcake" was first performed at the ChiSeries Very Special Christmas Special Special, 2010.

"The Sweater" was first performed at the 2nd Annual ChiSeries Very Special Christmas Special Special, 2011.

"Dreidel" was first performed at the ChiSeries Toronto Presents: A Very Special Hanukkah Special, 2012.

"Naughty" was first performed at the ChiSeries Toronto Presents: A Very Special Krampus Special, 2013.

"Special" was first performed at the ChiSeries Peterborough Presents: Speculating the Queer, 2014.

"Organ" was first performed at the ChiSeries Toronto Presents: A Very Special Saturnalia Special, 2014.

"Longest" was first performed at the ChiSeries Toronto Presents: A Very Special Winter Solstice Special, 2015.

"Green" is original to this collection.

All stories appear here in print for the first time.

ACKNOWLEDGEMENTS

I'd like to thank the founders of the Chiaroscuro Reading Series, Sandra Kasturi and Helen Marshall, for asking me to read at the very first ChiSeries Very Special Christmas Special Special, and all of the fans at ChiSeries Toronto who have looked forward to a new Derby Cavendish story every year since. Derby has a better voice because the stories were written to be read aloud.

I'd also like to thank ChiZine Publications co-publishers Brett Savory and Sandra Kasturi (again!) for bringing the Derby Cavendish stories together in a published collection; CZP managing editor Samantha Beiko for her excellent feedback and design; and artist Erik Mohr for a fabulous cover.

And as always, my special thanks to Ole Calderone for his love and his patience with a writer in the house.

ABOUT THE AUTHOR

Don Bassingthwaite is the author of numerous fantasy and dark fantasy novels, including The Dragon Below and Legacy of Dhakaan trilogies. His short stories have appeared in *Black Gate* magazine, *Imaginarium: The Best Canadian Speculative Fiction Writing*, and the Lambda Literary Award-winning *Bending the Landscape: Fantasy and Science Fiction* anthologies. He lives in Toronto with too many books, a well-stocked spice cupboard, and his partner.

EMB
RACE
THE
ODD